A check in his step had him pausing. She could feel the intensity of his gaze, marking her every feature even if she could not see his face.

Her mother and her cousin both exclaimed, and got to their feet. Like Genevieve, Gilliane started forward. Genevieve barely noticed. She reached him first and grasped for his hands.

They felt cold, cold as the grave, and they gripped Genevieve's with frantic strength. In one movement, he went down to his knee on the flagstone floor and tossed the hood back onto his shoulders.

She found herself staring into the face of a stranger.

Not Maddox. Not her friend at all. He could not be more unlike.

This man had dark hair, a profusion of curls that tumbled down his neck and over his brow. He had a narrow face bracketed by lines in the cheeks, though he could not be above a score and five. His eyes, too, were dark and burning with a kind of passion Genevieve had never before beheld.

"Lady Genevieve DeClare?"

Genevieve tried to recoil, but he held the hands she'd offered so eagerly, held them tight. Behind her, Gilliane cried out. Uncle Gervase exclaimed and started forward, but she could look nowhere save into those liquid dark eyes.

The Mistletoe Heart

by

Laura Strickland

Christmas in the Castle

The Mistletoe Heart

Cover Art by *Diana Carlile*

The Wild Rose Press, Inc.
PO Box 708
Adams Basin, NY 14410-0708
Visit us at www.thewildrosepress.com

Publishing History
First Edition, 2023
Trade Paperback ISBN 978-1-5092-4925-1
Digital ISBN 978-1-5092-4926-8

Christmas in the Castle
Published in the United States of America

Chapter One

Northern England, December 1190

Icy flakes of snow ticked against the mullion windows of the solar, and a cold draft swept across the floor, enough to set the flames on the candles dancing. Even here in this chamber, usually Genevieve DeClare's favorite refuge, the winter chill permeated, radiating right through the stone walls. Or perhaps the bitter bite she felt came of her own state of mind.

Desperate to focus on the duties at hand, she consulted the list in her mind of things to be done. Prepare the guest rooms. Make sure Cook had plenty of food to meet the increased demands of the season. Spread fresh rushes in the hall and ask the footmen to haul in the rest of the greenery.

The holy Christmas season was upon them, and much still needed to be done. Tomorrow was Christmas Eve. As soon as today, guests would begin arriving—family mostly—some from as far away as Scarborough and one, her aging Uncle Gervase, all the way from York.

She and her mother had spent weeks discussing whether or not they should hold any festivities this year. Always in the past, family had gathered here at the DeClare estate. Father had so enjoyed seeing the castle strewn with greenery, glowing with light and filled with song, and it had been a favorite time for Genevieve and her younger sister, Gilliane.

For the past six months, they had been a house in mourning. And they'd asked themselves over and over again: would it be deemed appropriate to celebrate this Christmas?

Genevieve knew what her dear father would have wanted. And mourning had to lessen, even if only gradually. She had watched her mother wither these past months, turning from a blooming rose to a pale shadow of the woman she had been, and Gilliane had grown so difficult Genevieve barely knew her. It would do them good to see family and those as close as family.

In the end, Genevieve had decided it for her mother's sake. If Mother kept failing, Genevieve feared she would lose her too, before spring. She had loved Father so much. They would honor his memory by trying to make it as joyous as they could.

Even if she, Genevieve, did not feel particularly joyous.

The weather, which had turned vile a week or more ago, seemed to echo her inner turmoil. It would make travel difficult for their guests. Some might not be able to reach the manor at all.

She walked to the window, breathed on a pane of glass, and tried to rub the frost away in order to peer out. Pinpricks of ice continued to strike the pane, making it difficult to see.

The solar lay directly above the hall, and the courtyard stretched below, wind-blown, mostly deserted, and dusted with snow. As she watched, Ralph, the stable boy, hastened across the yard, huddled against the cold.

"Genevieve, pray come away from that window. Do

you wish to take a chill?"

Genevieve swung around as her mother entered the chamber. Maude DeClare was a fragile and beautiful woman, and had been her husband's pride and joy. Genevieve had once heard him say he worked at all he did for the sake of his Maude. To be sure, he had made many improvements in the estate that had been in their family's possession since the first DeClare set foot on English soil. He had husbanded the lands well, which he believed included being good to their folk, and keeping good relations with their King, Richard.

Indeed, Father had been a fine man, and the love he'd given Mother had been a matter of great beauty. Genevieve had hoped for the same herself. Instead—

But no, she refused to think about that now, and pushed the memories from her mind. *A pair of earnest blue eyes. The whisper touch of warm lips. The mistletoe heart.*

"Mother, I am but fretting over the weather and hoping it will not spoil our plans."

"I have prayed on it, Genevieve. I believe all will be well."

Genevieve shot her mother a doubtful look. Mother had been spending far too much time in the chapel, which jutted from the side of the castle like the paw of a crouching cat.

"Is that where you have been? It is far too cold in there, Mother. Come, sit and get warm. Where is your shawl?"

Genevieve drew her mother to the bench in front of the fire, clutching the icy hands in her own. Mother smiled ruefully, though her pale gray eyes held no light. Genevieve had inherited those eyes, fringed by dark lashes, which she'd heard called beautiful. She'd gotten her dark hair, though, from Father, and proud she was to carry a part of him.

"I must have left the shawl somewhere. The chapel, perhaps."

Genevieve shed her own shawl and wrapped it around her mother's shoulders, which felt far too thin.

"There now. Would you like me to call for a warm drink?"

"Nay, Genevieve. Do not bother the kitchen. They are far too busy preparing for the—the festivities."

Mother's hesitation argued she felt as uncertain as Genevieve about this gathering. But Genevieve promised herself the company would do her good.

"Our guests may arrive late, but whatever the time, we will be ready for them."

"Have the DeVilles sent a message?"

"Not yet." Again, Genevieve glanced at the window. This would not be an easy holy day for the DeVilles, their closest neighbors. Nearly a year ago, their son Maddox had embarked upon a perilous journey and had not been heard from since.

A journey he'd undertaken at Genevieve's bidding.

She gave a sigh and tamped down the feelings that arose. Regret. Dread. Fear. Shame.

She and Maddox DeVille had grown up together, but a year apart in age. The two families were close, their fathers and mothers being good friends. It had always been expected they would one day join the estates together in the most natural of ways.

It was difficult when so many hearts embraced the same hope.

All but one.

Genevieve adored Maddox, as a friend. As a childhood companion grown into a fine and earnest man.

He admired her also, but far differently.

They had been thirteen and fourteen the first time Maddox declared himself. They'd been in the orchard on a fine summer's day, swinging on the lower branches of the apple trees, when he'd stilled suddenly and looked at her.

"Genevieve, you do know I want to marry you."

She'd stared. Even then she'd known it was what everyone expected. And even then, she'd known she should be grateful at having the opportunity to marry someone with whom she was so comfortable. Someone she knew would never treat her with coldness or cruelty.

And even then, she'd known she wanted a love like her parents shared, fully felt on both sides.

That little exchange in the orchard had altered their relationship, had at least changed the way she looked at Maddox. As subsequent days, months, and years flew by, she saw his love for her growing, while her feelings for him remained the same.

When she was seventeen and he eighteen, he and his father had ridden over to make a formal offer of marriage. They had met with Father who, by then, was already in the throes of his long illness.

He had called Genevieve in and made the proposal fairly.

By then, her older sister, Anora, was married and living at a distance. Genevieve understood her duty. She too must marry, as would Gilliane after her. Marriage to her best friend would not be a hard fate.

To everyone's surprise, she had refused the offer, saying merely that she was not yet ready to wed. She did not wish to hurt Maddox's feelings by rejecting him outright.

Since then, she'd come up with any number of excuses including a declaration she could not wed while Father was so ill. While her mother needed her at home.

Last Christmas, Maddox had approached her one more time. It had been a feast much like the one she now planned, only Father had been too ill to come down and join the company.

Maddox had caught Genevieve crying over it, right here in the solar. With infinite tenderness, he'd dried her tears and sought to provide comfort.

"Be of high heart, Genevieve. Only God knows when it is time for us to depart this life. Your father may still grow well."

Genevieve did not think so. They had consulted many physicians and attempted many remedies. She could feel her father slipping away.

Wretchedly, she had told Maddox, who was after all her best friend, "I do not think anything can save him."

He touched her cheek gently. She could still remember the expression in his clear, blue eyes. "List to me, Genevieve. Whatever happens to your father, you will not be forsaken. Accept me as your betrothed now. If you do, I will leave straight way on a pilgrimage. King Richard is in the Holy Land, fighting for the sacred city. I will join him, take prayers for your father's recovery, and offer them there. When I return—when I return, you and I can wed."

She should have said no. Though she believed in prayer, she didn't suppose it mattered where a prayer was offered. Still and all, Jerusalem was the holiest of cities. And the prayers would be offered by a young man who was pure of heart.

"How long would you be gone?"

He smiled at her, the sweet smile she'd known all her life. "I will be back by next Christmas."

A year. An entire year without the pressure of his suit hanging over her head. All she had to do was betroth herself to him, and she would be free for a year.

She should have said no. She'd said yes, instead.

His joy had been instant and boundless. There was nothing too great, so it seemed, for her to ask of him.

"Let us tell our parents, Gennie. They will be so happy. But first—"

They'd been standing near a branch of mistletoe. He'd towed her beneath it and taken a kiss, the first he'd ever had from her.

The last.

That kiss had been sad and sweet. Genevieve could feel his emotions, and guilt rose up inside her. She should prevent him going.

"It is a dangerous journey, Maddox."

"It is." His gaze never wavered from hers. "That does not matter." A slight smile crinkled his eyes. "Like a hero of old, Gennie, I will perform this quest for your sake."

"Then like a hero of old, you must have a token—to bring you luck. To keep you safe."

She'd reached up and snapped off a portion of the mistletoe, fashioning it swiftly into the shape of a heart.

To this she pressed her lips before presenting it to him. "This—this will keep you safe and whole."

Though now, a full year later, Genevieve wondered if it had.

Chapter Two

"Genevieve, do you have a moment?" Genevieve's young sister, Gilliane, put her head through the doorway of the solar and sought Genevieve's eyes. At fourteen, Gilliane was just beginning to claim the beauty she would later own. She stood as tall as Genevieve now, but her body remained whip-slim. She had Father's brown eyes and Mother's light-brown hair, and far more energy than she could easily contain.

"What is it, Gillie?" Genevieve asked. "I am very busy, as you know, arranging for our guests." Mother had gone down to the kitchens after getting warm by the fire. At least half of Genevieve's concern had followed her.

Gilliane came into the solar and gave Genevieve a demanding look. Father had always given his daughters—all three of them—a lot of leeway when it came to what they could do and say. Ofttimes they'd been allowed at the table with the grownups, especially during feast days, a tradition they still continued. Gilliane did not have a nurse, and her governess had gone home for Christmas before the weather turned bad.

Since Father's death, Gilliane had become what Genevieve could only call obstreperous. She questioned her sister's decisions and tended to argue with whatever she was told. Genevieve figured it must be her way of dealing with the loss of Father who, like everyone else,

Gilliane had adored. Not wanting her mother troubled, Genevieve had done all she could to deal with her sister, but given the present circumstances her patience was wearing thin.

"When will our guests arrive?" Gilliane asked with an edge in her voice.

"Soon, I hope. The roads are bad, and it's snowing again. I'm hoping Uncle Gervase and Cousin Agnes can make the journey at all. If you want something to do," Genevieve suggested pointedly, "you might go to the chapel and offer prayers for their safety."

"It is cold in the chapel. Will the DeVilles come?" Lord Hugh and Lady Joan DeVille were Maddox's parents, their closest neighbors.

"You know they will. Lord Hugh, Lady Joan, and Eduard also." Eduard was Maddox's younger brother, and as little like him as Gilliane was like herself. Genevieve had wondered for a time if in a few years Gilliane and Eduard might make a match. There appeared to be nothing but animosity between them, however. And though Gilliane had tried valiantly to hide it, Genevieve had long since guessed that Gilliane held a *tendresse* for Maddox. It showed in the way her face lit up when he entered a room or teased her in the kind, brotherly way he had.

She had of course never charged Gilliane with her suspicions. Young ladies had a right to a measure of privacy when it came to what lay in their hearts. And who could blame any female for favoring Maddox?

"I pray you will strive to get along and be docile and accommodating while they are here. I understand we have lost much, but I wish for Mother to have an enjoyable holy season."

Gilliane's brown eyes, lit by specks of gold—or mischief—met Genevieve's. "Am I not always accommodating?"

"Nay, I have to say you are not."

"That shows what you know." Gilliane sniffed. "Father never complained about me." For an instant, the bright eyes dimmed with grief.

"He never complained about any of us." Father had done his best to find Anora a good and steady husband, even if she did not know him aforehand and had to go all the way to Somerset to live. Hector was young, not unpleasant to look upon, and the lord of wealthy lands. Of good blood also, as Mother often noted.

Perhaps, Genevieve thought now, Father had been overly fond. It might have been better had he found fault with his daughters a time or two. Now he was gone, and Gilliane was very nearly out of hand.

"All I am saying," she beseeched her sister, "is try to get along while our guests are here. Be quiet and complimentary. Say only nice things, do not—as you so frequently do—point out what is amiss with a person or a situation."

"I do not do that."

Genevieve just gazed at Gilliane.

Gilliane sniffed. "Well, if people would be what they should be, I would not find so much fault." She hesitated, and took another turn around the chamber. "Speaking of such—" She turned suddenly and faced Genevieve full on, "do you think Maddox will come?"

This, as Genevieve saw all at once, had been the true reason for Gilliane seeking her out. She inquired about Maddox's parents, aye, because she understood why they were spending the holy season here at Clarendon.

Maddox had promised to return by this Christmas. Tomorrow was Christmas Eve.

Genevieve sat on the bench she'd so recently shared with Mother, and patted the place beside her. "Come, Gilliane." How best to broach this? Like many a young girl, Gilliane had dreams, she imagined. In her most secret heart, had they included Maddox?

Gilliane's expression turned mutinous. She stayed where she was. "Do you think he will return?" A sharp wisdom flickered in Gilliane's eyes. "Do you want him to?"

"Of course I do." Genevieve was half sick with worry for Maddox. With remorse. With the desire to see him safe and well. Even—even if that meant their marriage must then move forward. "Why would you suppose differently?"

"I do not know. Sometimes I can feel things about people. About the way you feel for him."

Genevieve's face heated. She held hard to her composure. What could a girl of fourteen understand of the twisted threads of love and obligation?

She said softly, "Maddox is my best friend."

"And your betrothed." Now the angry color came to Gillian's cheeks. "I do not see why he ever looked only at you."

"We were friends from very young—"

"I know that," Gilliane interrupted her. "But if you ask me, he deserves better."

Genevieve stifled a sigh. "I do hope Maddox arrives sometime between now and Three Kings Day. It is the greatest wish of my heart."

"Because you love him."

"I do, yes."

"Then," Gilliane pushed, "if you love Maddox so much, why did you send him away?"

The very question that had haunted Genevieve this past twelve-month. "For Father's sake. It was hard to see Maddox go. A long separation. But Gillie, you have to understand, Maddox offered to make the pilgrimage. He chose to go. I did not send him." She denied it, even to her own heart.

"I do not agree. He went because you said when he returned, the two of you would marry." Now tears flooded Gilliane's eyes, though they looked like tears of anger. "You could have kept him safe at home. What if something has happened to him?"

Aye, what if something had?

"Maddox is young and strong, and has a household guard riding with him. What could happen?"

"A thousand things. Attacks by Saracens. Falling victim to the fighting. Hostile lands through which he must travel—"

Aye, all those things.

"And…" Two tears overflowed and made tracks down Gilliane's cheeks. "And Father died anyway! So what good did it do?"

"I know, lamb. I know." If only. If only Maddox's earnest prayers could have saved Father. If only Maddox would ride in tonight, or tomorrow, or any time during the next twelve days.

"So you sent him for nothing!" It was a howl. "And you are selfish. That is something Father taught us never to be."

"I say to you again, Gilliane, I did not send Maddox—"

"But you did not prevent him going. And you could

have. It would have taken but a word from you. He would have done anything you asked."

Truth, again. And something with which Genevieve must strive to live.

"I just wish Maddox was not alone out there"—Gilliane waved an arm at the windows—"in that wide world. And more than anything, I wish he would come home."

So did Genevieve.

Chapter Three

Lord Hugh and Lady Joan DeVille, with their son Eduard, arrived just before sunset, complaining about the vile roads.

"We had not far to travel, thank goodness," Sir Hugh said as the maid took his cloak. Genevieve knew as much—she could run the distance between their manor houses in no time and had done so often, barefoot.

"We got stuck once and nearly so again. There is ice on the roads, and the wind is devilish strong."

"Ice?" Mother looked unhappy. "I hoped 'twas but snow. My brother, Gervase, is supposed to be coming from York. It is so far, but I would much love to see him."

Hugh DeVille took Mother's hands. "I am certain he will persevere, dear lady, though he may well arrive late."

"Aye, and my niece also, with her husband and children. They were so dear to my William." Her voice broke over Father's name. "I am afraid that is all we are expecting, with dear Maddox still away."

This time Lady Joan, Maddox's mother, lowered her eyes. "Aye. 'Twill be a somber Christmas withal."

Young Eduard, all of sixteen years now he must be, made a sound in his throat but did not comment. He had grown since Genevieve had last seen him. She had not been visiting the DeVille estate as often, with Maddox

14

away.

Now he had shot up to near Maddox's height, though, save for his fair hair, he looked as little like his brother as Gilliane looked like Genevieve. Now he wore a sulky, unhappy expression. No wonder he and Gilliane did not get along. They were both strong-willed and stubborn.

He shot a glare at Genevieve, and she turned away. Did Maddox's parents and brother blame her for his absence, just like Gilliane? Did they hate her for sending him away?

"Maddox is here in spirit," Lord DeVille said, "as is William, for all that."

"Come closer to the fire." Genevieve ushered them in, summoned the maid to serve them drinks, and did her best to enliven the conversation.

For all her best efforts, however, the conversation limped along. Though they tried hard, no one felt merry, and it did not take long for Gilliane and Eduard to begin pecking at one another. Their relationship seemed too much like family for their elders to correct them, though eventually Lord Hugh did come down upon his son, with a warning to mind his manners.

By then, everyone was tired, and Genevieve showed her guests up to bed.

Later, though, alone in her chamber when Mother and even the servants lay safe in their own cots, she stared into the dark and thought of Maddox, her best friend. With the sunny smile and the laugh that made you want to laugh also.

Her betrothed. Because they were that, betrothed.

If he came back now, if he walked through the door tomorrow, she would be glad to see him, more than she could express. She would fall to her knees in gratitude. But would she want to marry him? She should. He was her best friend.

But not her love.

Mayhap she did not deserve a love like Mother's and Father's. A young woman who would send away a young man so fine and earnest as Maddox DeVille—why, she deserved no blessings.

There in her cold bed, she curled into a tight ball. Outside, the snow still fell. She sent her mind wandering through it, over hills marked with white and southward, south and west to places she could scarce imagine.

Through the fields of Europe to the burning heat of the Holy Land. So far, so far away. Where could he be? She'd missed him over the past year, missed his company far more than she'd expected.

Her dearest friend.

In her bed, she squeezed her eyes tight shut. The tears leaked through anyway. She must be strong for Mother's sake, and for the sake of Maddox's family. She must keep hope alive that Maddox would yet return.

****

The following day, Christmas Eve, the weather eased and the rest of the guests arrived. Cousin Agnes and her family, from Scarborough, had terrible tales to tell of the roads and seemed vastly grateful to have arrived warm and safe at Clarendon.

Genevieve gave herself over to supplying their every comfort. To seeing to the guest chambers yet again, giving orders for the fires to be lit. If she lost herself in doing for others, perhaps it would ease the pain in her own heart.

Uncle Gervase, who had traveled all the way from

York, declared he'd almost turned back several times and had arrived only because of the courage of his valiant driver. Genevieve immediately sent the half-frozen man to the servants' hall for rest and a warm drink.

Cousin Agnes's two young children soon livened up proceedings, chasing with Father's old wolfhound, Rex.

Lastly came the harper Genevieve had hired for the season, Master Dennis, who had traveled on foot and looked chilled to the very bones.

It was everyone Genevieve expected, and she breathed a sigh of relief. She made an opportunity to step out to the chapel, where she lit a candle and gave a prayer of gratitude. She also said a prayer for Maddox's safety, wherever he might be.

The Christmas Eve feast proved a success. The boards fairly groaned beneath the food, and the conversation sang. Genevieve heard her mother laugh, for the first time in half a year, over something Uncle Gervase said.

Aye, this was what Mother needed to lift her spirits and take her from the dark place she'd inhabited since Father's passing. Keeping Christmas this year had been the right thing to do after all.

After the meal, Master Dennis tuned up his harp and began to play, with the younger members of the company dancing to his tunes, and Genevieve had just begun to relax, listening to the enchanting music, when there came a great pounding at the outer door. She leaped up and heard voices coming from that direction—the footman, John, greeting whoever had arrived.

Lady Joan started up also, and her gaze met Genevieve's across the table. Blue her eyes were and so like her son's it made Genevieve shiver.

At that moment, she knew she and Lady Joan entertained the very same thought: *Maddox*.

Had he come? Was it possible he might return tonight? By next Christmas, he'd said. And that could mean today.

She should go running out. She should hurry to see. But her feet remained rooted to the flagstones.

She heard the footman say, "This way, sir." And footsteps. A man's footsteps. Someone approached the hall.

It must be him.

Rex gave a bark. Genevieve's heart leaped, quivered in her breast, and half strangled her. Eyes now fixed on the wide doorway, and with one hand pressed to her throat, she waited.

The figure that appeared looked tall and much too broad to be Maddox. But then, he wore a heavy cloak, its shoulders pattered with snow, and men often looked bigger clad so. He also had the hood raised over his hair so Genevieve could not see the gleam of honey-gold locks that always made her think of sunlight.

Sudden joy pounded through her. *Maddox. Home.* She wanted nothing more than for it to be true.

She started forward, ignoring the footman, who shot her a look of—was that warning? Her hands were already outstretched for Maddox's when they met in the center of the room. Because he was above all else her friend. Come home.

A check in his step had him pausing. She could feel the intensity of his gaze, marking her every feature even if she could not see his face.

Her mother and her cousin both exclaimed, and got to their feet. Like Genevieve, Gilliane started forward.

Genevieve barely noticed. She reached him first and grasped for his hands.

They felt cold, cold as the grave, and they gripped Genevieve's with frantic strength. In one movement, he went down to his knee on the flagstone floor and tossed the hood back onto his shoulders.

She found herself staring into the face of a stranger.

Not Maddox. Not her friend at all. He could not be more unlike.

This man had dark hair, a profusion of curls that tumbled down his neck and over his brow. He had a narrow face bracketed by lines in the cheeks, though he could not be above a score and five. His eyes, too, were dark and burning with a kind of passion Genevieve had never before beheld.

"Lady Genevieve DeClare?"

Genevieve tried to recoil, but he held the hands she'd offered so eagerly, held them tight. Behind her, Gilliane cried out. Uncle Gervase exclaimed and started forward, but she could look nowhere save into those liquid dark eyes.

"Sir? Who are you? How do you know me?"

His gaze touched every feature of her face—brow, cheekbones, lips. "I would know you anywhere."

His fingers warmed where they gripped hers, and began to heat her flesh. The sensation crept upward in contrast to the chill of alarm she felt.

"My name, it is Tomas Monmercy." He had an accent, a fluid one that warmed his words. "Maddox DeVille has sent me."

Genevieve's knees wobbled. "Maddox? Where is he?"

"Not with me. I come in his stead. He bade me

journey to you."

"What is all this?" Uncle Gervase stepped up and took Genevieve's elbow. "Sirrah, what is the meaning of your presence here?"

The stranger released Genevieve's fingers and got slowly to his feet. He gazed around at those gathered in the hall, who now without exception all stared at him.

"I am Tomas Monmercy," he repeated to Gervase, "friend to Maddox DeVille." His accent made the names sing. "Maddox and I met during a battle, in Jerusalem. I greatly regret to tell you all that he is dead."

Maddox's mother gave a cry, and despite Uncle Gervase's support, Genevieve's legs gave way. She sank to the floor.

No! It could not be true. And if true, it was her fault. She it was who had sent Maddox on his way. Never, if this knight could be believed, to return.

Tomas Monmercy knelt again, so that he faced Genevieve, barely an arm's reach away. Intently, he repeated, "He sent me to you. He charged me with the journey as he lay dying. He begged me, my lady Genevieve, to bring you this."

Reaching inside his tunic, he extracted a small packet of silk. Not a sound broke the silence of the chamber as he unfolded it and offered the contents to Genevieve, on the palm of his hand.

She saw—oh, dear God, it was the mistletoe heart. The one she had fastened with such haste, last Christmas, and given to Maddox as a token. That he'd intended to bring back to her.

It looked the worse for wear, frayed and tattered, all the berries fallen away. As fragile as what had lain between them.

"My lady, my duty is done." And Tomas Monmercy placed the relic in her hand.

Chapter Four

They had provided Tomas a guest chamber, this family, the friends of Maddox DeVille. Despite their grief and their all-too-visible shock and misery, they had. As a friend and former companion of their beloved Maddox, he was made welcome.

He would expect no less of Maddox's people. The man had himself been the very definition of warmth and generosity.

Tomas surveyed the chamber to which a footman had shown him without truly seeing it. In nearly two years he had not experienced such simple comforts. One did not find them on the trail to or from the Holy Land, nor while fighting there. And although he'd wanted to go home—had ached for it while in confinement—he had not dared veer from the task to which he'd been charged on Maddox's behalf.

What a nightmare that journey had been. Challenge upon challenge, including skirmishes all along the way, a missed ship across the Channel, and the second ship nearly going down in bad weather. It had taken him days riding north, and this vile storm at the end of it.

"*Mais, mon ami*, I have done as you asked."

He hoped the task of returning the heart would provide Maddox with peace. The young man had certainly been deserving of that. Whether or not he had brought Mistress Genevieve any measure of peace, he could not tell.

He crossed to the window and tried to peer out but could see only darkness, lit by tiny blobs of white. The storm with which the good Lord had challenged the end of his journey still raged.

No matter. He was safe and warm, a state he had not enjoyed in far too long. He could put the rest of it away from him.

Except—the images continually flooded his mind. The bright, burning sun of the Holy Land. The flash of light on clashing arms. The banners, the blood and death.

Men went to fight in the Holy Land for many reasons. Some out of zeal and devotion. Some, as he suspected, from obligation. And some—some to earn a place in Heaven and thus everlasting life.

He'd encountered enough men of the latter ilk during his time there. Tough, hardened men who bragged that henceforth they might do whatever they chose, break any commandment, because they'd bought their way to everlasting glory.

Maddox DeVille had been different. From the first Tomas met him, he'd been able to tell that. Maddox had not been in Jerusalem to fight but to carry out a holy mission. There had not been a speck of spite or ugliness in him.

He had not deserved his fate.

With a grunt, Tomas removed his boots, wondering when he had last done so, and with a groan he lay down on the bed. Such comfort! His battered body sank into the wool batting of the mattress, and he relaxed the merciless thoughts in his mind.

An image, a single image, appeared there instead. The face of Genevieve DeClare.

Maddox had not lied about her—no, he certainly had not. Truly, Tomas would not have expected that young man to lie. An angel, Maddox had called her, and *oui*, she had the face of *l'ange*.

A smooth brow marked by dark, faintly arched brows, a straight, elegant nose, and lips like pink roses. Maddox had said she had twin dimples when she smiled.

She had not smiled at Tomas.

Those eyes—ah, those eyes. Incomparable. *You can see Genevieve's thoughts in her eyes,* Maddox had said. *And sometimes her soul also. She has the most beautiful soul.*

She did not know it, but Mistress Genevieve and Maddox's descriptions of her had kept the both of them alive. Maddox had not come to the Holy Land to fight, no, but King Richard's campaign had been in full spate when he'd arrived, and he'd got caught up in it.

Tomas's company, though from Brittany, had been attached to King Richard's forces when Tomas and Maddox met.

It had been in the midst of a skirmish on a hot summer's day, as far from the present place and time as could be.

"Get out of the way, *monsieur*," Tomas remembered shouting at the fair-haired stranger.

"I must get through!"

Amid the crashing, the sweat, and the blood, Tomas had focused on Maddox's face. A young face it had seemed and an earnest one, the blue eyes fervent.

"Where are you trying to go?"

"To the Church of the Holy Sepulcher," the young man had gasped. "I must offer prayers there."

He had never made it. Even as they spoke together,

the battle had exploded around them. Tomas, who had dismounted to speak to the earnest pilgrim, had been separated from his horse, Algernon, and his company.

Right up until the end, Maddox had regretted that. He had mourned the fact that having traveled all that way in order to offer prayers for healing, meant for the father of the woman he loved, he had failed in his mission.

Tomas's fingers curled into fists, driven by frustration. If he could change things for Maddox even now, he would. But they had both been taken prisoner that day, taken together. And the only prayers Maddox had been able to offer had sounded in a barren cell.

A full month they'd been held. At least, Tomas figured it for a month, though to be truthful, he'd lost count. Day and night were much the same there. There had been punishments aimed at making them renounce their faith. Tomas still bore the scars. Maddox had withstood that as well as he. There had been a dearth of food, and precious little water. Other than that, only one another's company.

They had spoken of many things. Their childhoods—both mostly happy. Tomas's experiences growing up as a younger son even as Maddox was an elder, one who had no vocation for the cloth. Maddox had spoken mostly of his love, Genevieve. Of uncounted, sunlit days spent with her when they were children. Of her kindness, her humor, her beauty.

Non, he had not lied about that.

He'd painted pictures with his words, there in that barren cell, so vivid and true that Tomas could see the woman. And he too began to fall a little bit in love with her.

When, at length, Tomas's commander, Herbert

DeFougeres, had negotiated his release, Tomas had refused to leave the prison without Maddox. Herbert had bargained for him also, and since Saladin had a surfeit of other prisoners, he had relented.

But it had been too late for Maddox by then. He must have caught the fever in the dungeons. It took him swiftly and it took him hard, there in the sweltering summer of Jerusalem.

Tomas had intended to have Maddox carried to the Church of the Holy Sepulcher so he could offer his prayers. There had been no time. Not two days later, Maddox had died in Tomas's arms.

His last words had been, "Return it to her, Tomas. Take to my Genevieve the mistletoe heart."

"I will."

"Tell her I regret—regret having failed her."

"*Mon ami*, you have failed no one."

"Promise me."

"It is my vow to you. I will return to her this treasure. Now you must rest and grow strong."

He'd been gone already, his earnest gaze wide and still focused on Tomas's, his skin burning hot. There had been nothing to do but close his eyes and whisper a prayer.

Nothing to do but keep his vow.

Sir Herbert was a merciful man, and a godly one. He'd given Tomas permission to remain with his ailing friend until he died, and to leave after that to complete the sacred mission with which Maddox had charged him. And now that he had presented the token to Maddox's beautiful betrothed? Having beheld Genevieve's beauty, what came next for him?

Chapter Five

Christmas Day had arrived, the Christmas of a year that had brought much uncertainty and unimaginable loss.

Genevieve sat at her dressing table where she should be bundling her hair—her maid being busy with preparations downstairs—up under her veil. She had no hope, however, of focusing on the task or getting her thoughts away from—

Maddox. Dead in the Holy Land. Where she, Genevieve, had sent him.

Such a scene in the hall last evening after Sir Tomas had been shown up to his chamber! Poor Lady Joan had been prostrated, and who could blame her? She had sobbed in Lord Hugh's arms, weeping her son's name over and over again. Young Eduard had worn a look on his face such as Genevieve had never before seen. It looked as if someone had punched him hard in the chest. Gilliane appeared both shocked and angry, and Sir Hugh had gone pure white.

Mother, too, had sobbed. Aye, Maddox had been like a son to Mother, and this was the second hard loss she'd endured in a year. Even the children, Justin and Emmaline, had gone silent, and old Rex had lain with his head on his paws.

And Genevieve? How had she felt? Ah, it went beyond expression.

Now she sat here at her dressing table, not knowing how she would face this day. Her combs and brushes lay untouched. In her hand, resting on the narrow palm as it had on Tomas Monmercy's broad one last night, lay the mistletoe heart.

A thing, a mere trinket fashioned with haste and bestowed on impulse. One that had quite clearly meant very much to Maddox. It had journeyed with him to Jerusalem, a place she would never see.

He had made the hard journey, and its effects showed on the heart in her hand. Frayed, as she'd remarked last evening. Fair crumbling.

His heart had been so true. Why could she not have loved him, if only for that? Loved him as he deserved.

She should get up and go downstairs. Many tasks awaited her. Lady Joan, informed so abruptly about the death of her son, would need care and comfort.

She must provide for their uninvited guest also, offer to have the servants fill a bath for him, though the poor serving men were already run off their feet. It was the holy season, and charity must be respected. Besides—

Besides, this man, this Tomas Monmercy, had been most kind in bringing word, and the trinket, to her.

Before anything else, she should go to the chapel. Speak a prayer. Sue for peace.

And forgiveness.

She had sent Maddox on a journey, one he'd undertaken for love of her, that had cost him his life.

A single tear fell and wetted the tattered object in her hand. Swiftly, she laid it aside.

It needed no further damage from her salt tears.

A soft knock sounded at her door. It opened and her mother peeked in.

"How are you, my dear?"

"Come in, Mother, please."

Maude DeClare entered and sat down across from Genevieve, studying her face worriedly.

"You look tired, Daughter."

"I did not sleep."

"No wonder. I have myself wept most the night. To think of that sweet boy, who undertook that pilgrimage on your dear father's behalf, perishing so far from home."

Nay, on *her* behalf. "Have you seen Lady Joan this morning? How is she?"

"Not at all well. Both she and Sir Hugh are heartbroken." Mother twisted her hands in her lap. "I would not be surprised if they fail to stay until Three Kings Day but decide to go home."

"How is the weather this morning?"

"Still blowing, I am afraid. Honestly, I do not know how Sir Tomas made his way hence last night, especially in the dark. Perhaps God's angels guided him."

When Genevieve said nothing, her mother touched her cheek. "Whatever you may think now, Genevieve, Sir Tomas's arrival was a blessing. 'Tis better to know of Maddox's fate than to keep waiting upon his return."

"Aye."

"Would you like me to dress your hair for you? You used to love that when you were small. Then we will go to the chapel together before we tend to our guests."

Genevieve merely nodded, not trusting herself to speak. The long strokes of the comb and of her mother's hands felt soothing. But she did not think she could ever ease this rampant pain she felt.

****

They encountered Tomas Monmercy on his way out of the chapel. He wore the same heavy cloak in which he had arrived last night, but with the hood back upon his broad shoulders and his dark head bared. His step checked when he saw them.

"My lady DeClare, Mistress Genevieve. I wish you a joyous morning."

There was very little joy to be found, Genevieve thought, but she returned the greeting.

Mother spoke warmly. "I see you have found our chapel."

"I was directed here most kindly by your footman. I wished only to say a prayer and light a candle." He switched his dark gaze to Genevieve's face. "For Maddox. I have done so at every church I passed all the long way from Jerusalem."

A most pious man, Genevieve thought. Or perhaps merely a very good friend.

"I hope you will go in and take your breakfast," Mother said. "We will also speak our prayers and join you."

He nodded and with one last look at Genevieve went on his way.

The interior of the chapel felt cold as a tomb. In addition to the usual votive lights, only Tomas's candle burned.

Genevieve went to her knees before the altar and closed her eyes.

She'd been told all her life that her God was a merciful God. She'd always believed it. She'd had kind parents, a good roof over her head, and unlike so many, plenty to eat. She'd had a best friend.

Now she did not know what to ask of a merciful

God. Forgiveness? Comfort she did not deserve?

"Sustain me," she whispered and continued to kneel until her limbs went numb.

"Come, Daughter."

Mother's hand drew her up. Curious, how Genevieve had been the strong one since Father's death, and now her mother offered her support.

At the door of the chapel, she faltered and gazed into her mother's face.

"Mother, how shall I ever endure it?"

"It is insupportable, I know. We live on faith that dear Maddox is in a peaceful place beyond the pain and troubles of this world."

Did Mother truly believe that? Then why had she shed so many tears for Father who, presumably, also now inhabited Heaven?

"Come. Let us tend to our guests."

Mother chatted on as they returned to the hall, saying it was good to have tasks and household matters to occupy one's mind. True, Genevieve supposed, only her mind did not seem to be working aright. She struggled just to order her thoughts.

Uncle Gervase came forward to meet them when they entered the hall. "Come, Sister, Niece. You sit. All is in readiness."

The cousins from Scarborough were already in attendance, the children, allowed into the hall during this holiday session, tucking into their breakfasts. Genevieve's cousin, Agnes—Uncle Gervase's daughter—and her husband, Roger, appeared uncomfortable.

Maddox's father also sat at table, though his mother had not come down.

Genevieve greeted him with concern. "Is Lady Joan unwell, Lord Hugh?"

"She is not handling the word we had last evening very easily."

Tomas Monmercy looked up from his place at the table. "Monsieur, I regret being the bearer of such sad tidings."

"Nay, sirrah." Lord Hugh bowed. "We are in your debt. 'Tis better to possess the truth, however painful."

Uncle Gervase escorted Genevieve to a chair beside Gilliane, who did not so much as glance at her. Genevieve could feel the anger pouring from her sister. There was one person besides herself, it seemed, who blamed Genevieve for Maddox's fate.

She turned to Sir Tomas. "Can you tell us when?" she asked. "When did Maddox perish?"

His eyes flew up from his trencher and he regarded her gravely. "Mistress Genevieve, I will provide you any comfort I may, and answer any questions you wish. Perhaps, however, we should wait—"

"Just one question. Answer me that one."

"Monsieur Maddox perished late in the month of July—the hottest part of the year there in Jerusalem."

The same as Father. Genevieve shot her mother a look. Her hands began to tremble violently.

"I am sorry." Tomas Monmercy spoke softly. "Am I to understand that your father, Lord William DeClare, did not recover from his illness? Maddox told me all about it, you see. His quest and—and the reasons behind it."

"Now they rest together in eternity," said Cousin Agnes piously.

"Indeed," said Uncle Gervase, but he did not appear

comforted.

Tomas Monmercy leaned toward Genevieve across the boards. "After breakfast, I have promised to go to Lady DeVille and share with her all I can about her son. His bravery. His—his brilliance of spirit. I hope, Mistress Genevieve, you will do me the honor of sitting with me when you feel able, that I might do the same for you."

"Aye," was all Genevieve could manage. She would listen to everything her heart could bear.

Chapter Six

Tomas Monmercy spent more than an hour with Maddox's mother and father in their guest chamber. Genevieve marked the passing of the time, keeping an eye on the water clock that had been Father's pride and joy.

He must indeed have much to say. Details, no doubt, of Maddox's journey. Of their conversations. Of all that had befallen him.

She kept an eye on the stairs and noticed that Gilliane did also, when not occupied with shooting resentful looks at her. A storm was brewing there, and no mistake. Lately Gilliane had experienced difficulty with keeping her emotions in check. Genevieve imagined it would not take long for her to set an attack.

Young Eduard, on the other hand, seemed closed in and overly quiet. The news of his brother's passing had clearly hit him hard, yet he retained his usual sulky look. It could not be easy for the lad, so Genevieve told herself, with his mother shut into a guest chamber, and his father in attendance there.

Genevieve was helping her young cousins strew additional greenery around the hall, though her heart was not in it, when Sir Tomas returned. He came in with his head bowed and deep sadness in his eyes.

Genevieve drew out a chair for him, away from the others. "Please sit. May I bring you a mug of ale?"

Instead of answering, he gazed into her face. His eyes seemed to measure her, to peer beneath the skin to what might not be so easily seen.

"Forgive me staring, Mistress Genevieve. You are just how Maddox described you. Indeed, he gave such an exacting picture, I feel I knew you before ever we met."

A lump formed in Genevieve's throat. "How did he describe me?"

"Kind. Warm. Generous. Here you prove it. Victim of your own grief, you nevertheless worry for the comfort of a poor traveler."

Heat flooded Genevieve's skin. "It is naught."

"It is a great deal. Maddox deeply admired as well as loved you. I dare say he lived and breathed for your sake."

"Pray, Sir Tomas, do not—"

"I am sorry. My words serve merely to intensify your grief."

In ways he could not possibly understand.

"Let me get you that ale. Or perhaps some mulled cider."

'Please, no. Sit down with me."

She perched on the bench opposite his chair, mostly because her legs did not want to hold her.

"Why did you choose that one question for me this morning, of when Maddox had died?"

Genevieve shook her head. "I merely wondered. I could not rid myself of the notion that, as Maddox had gone to the Holy Land to pray for Father's recovery, they might perhaps have perished at the same time."

"And they did," he said softly.

"They did."

"Mistress Genevieve, Maddox deeply regretted that

he was unable to offer the prayers your father needed before he succumbed to the fever." Tomas's eyes held a look of questioning. "He rued it most tremendously, even to his dying breath."

Oh God. Oh, God!

"I hope you will not think," Tomas went on a bit awkwardly, "that your father perished because Maddox failed to complete his pilgrimage as he would have done, I have no doubt, had we not been captured. And after we were freed—"

Genevieve was not sure what she thought. "No guilt lies with Maddox, most certainly."

"I am very glad to hear you say so. For you to have thought badly of him, it would have broken his heart."

"The two of you became very good friends."

Tomas shrugged. "Many linger in Saladin's prisons. We two happened to be in the same cell, a space no greater in length than my two arms outstretched. We had little to do but talk."

"Was it a terribly harsh place, this prison?"

Again his eyes seemed to measure her gravely. "The description of it is not fit for your ears."

How close had that encouraged Maddox and Sir Tomas to become? Genevieve wondered. Two young men under terrible duress.

She got abruptly to her feet. "Let me get you that draught of ale. And I would like to offer for my servants to prepare you a bath. I will ask the men to carry water up to your chamber."

"I would very much appreciate that."

She clasped her hands together. "And I want to say, I hope you will do us the honor of spending the Christmas season here. My uncle and cousins plan on staying until Three Kings Day. I hope you will consider doing the same."

"*Merci.*"

"Unless—unless you are anxious to return to your own family. In France?"

"Brittany. I am in no hurry, at least not before the weather turns better for traveling."

"Fine then. Let me go and organize it."

Genevieve turned and walked away. Being in Tomas Monmercy's presence shook her. Even as she walked from the hall, she admitted that to herself. The way he looked at her did, respectful but somehow intimate. Perhaps that was the way men in Brittany regarded women. She had heard it was a rustic place.

She went about her scores of tasks, but her thoughts hovered there with the man, haunted by his grave, dark eyes.

****

Following the lengthy conversation with Sir Tomas, Lord Hugh DeVille announced that he, Maddox's mother, and young Eduard would be unable to stay until Three Kings Day and were ready to return, as soon as the morrow, to their own estate. The weather, however, kept them at Clarendon.

Genevieve learned from the servants that Sir Tomas had inquired after the welfare of his horse and been assured the destrier was safe and well looked after in the stables.

The footmen, sweaty but not complaining, dragged untold numbers of buckets up to his chamber. The harper played most the afternoon, though only the children, Justin and Emmaline, had much heart for merriment and dancing.

A grand feast with no less than seven courses was planned for Christmas night. A goose had been killed, and Genevieve had raided the larder mercilessly. While planning, she had pinned her hopes on lifting everyone's spirits high and making a difference for her mother.

Now it all seemed a waste. How could she be joyful with Lady Joan shut into her chamber, with both Gilliane and Eduard glowering—often at each other? With Maddox on her mind?

At least the servants would enjoy a feast of their own in their hall. She would be sure to tell them to take what they wished of the food, and perhaps she could lend them the harper's services for a time. They had more than earned it, doing double duty this past year and helping to keep the estate running. And they too missed Father, who had ever been good to them.

She went to the kitchen and spoke with Cook, who along with her three maids tended a plethora of pots. Cook looked harried and her cheeks glowed bright red, but she put everything aside when she saw Genevieve.

"Mistress?"

"I think, Cora, we are the same number, plus one with Sir Tomas here, for tonight's feast. Lord and Lady DeVille are ready to leave, but I do not believe they will attempt that until morning."

Cook clucked her tongue. "I do not doubt it. And ye, Mistress? How be ye holding up?"

At the kind and simple words, tears pricked the backs of Genevieve's eyes. "I am focusing on providing everyone else a fine Christmas."

"Aye, Mistress." Sympathy warmed Cook's gaze. The three maids had paused and stood watching.

"I am sorry…" Genevieve began and faltered before

starting again. "I am sorry you have had so much work and no one now in the mood to celebrate. Please take what you will for your feast. We are so few, and there will be more than enough."

"Bless ye, Mistress. Master Maddox was a fine young man. Why, I've known him from a wee lad, and him here as often as he was at home."

"That is true."

"I have shed a few tears myself. But it is Christmas still, and we should keep it."

"Aye."

"Thank ye, Mistress, for your generosity."

Genevieve nodded and went out. She met her cousin, Agnes, in the corridor.

Agnes had a plain, pretty face now wreathed in concern. "Genevieve, Roger bade me ask if you would prefer for us to leave. I know we were meant to stay until Three Kings Day, but—"

"Oh, goodness, pray do not do that. Maddox's parents already speak of going home."

"I know. We heard. That is why we thought—well, you will not be in any frame of mind to entertain, will you? And 'tis difficult to explain things to the children. They know only that 'tis Christmas, and they will try and run about."

"Oh, mercy." Genevieve thought about what the castle would be like if her cousin, her husband, and their lively children departed. Quiet as the grave. Even if Uncle Gervase stayed, well, he was a man with a quiet disposition, and she could not expect Tomas to keep long from returning home, whatever he said.

Impulsively she told Agnes, "Do stay. 'Twould be so very bleak without you."

"I wonder when Lord Hugh and Lady Joan plan to leave."

"'Twill depend upon the weather. It still rages out there. At least they do not have far to go, unlike you, who must travel all the way to Scarborough. Only think of the roads."

"Aye, well, if the children become too fractious, just drop a word in my ear."

"They are not fractious, Cousin. It is good to hear their laughter."

"And you," Agnes placed her arm around Genevieve's shoulders. "If there is aught I may do to lighten your burden—"

"Pray, Cousin, do not spare so much as a thought for me."

Chapter Seven

Tomas eased himself down into the steaming water with a groan. The copper tub was a deep one and had required many trips up and down the back stairs to fill. But oh, what bliss!

He had fantasized about just this the entire time he was in the Holy Land. Had longed for it, even as his body acquired a plethora of small wounds, all adding up to debilitate him. As the sand and the sweat entered every crack of his skin, so he could taste them.

As he and Maddox suffered and bled together in their filthy prison.

Now one of the two brawny footmen who'd carried up the water stood by, eyeing him.

"Do ye need anything else, my lord? Only, with all the festivities, I am needed downstairs."

"Go. And thank you."

The man nodded and left. Tomas slid farther down into the water, so it lapped around his neck, and began to relax.

How long since he had been at his ease? He could scarce remember. It had been a privilege being chosen to accompany Herbert DeFougeres to the Holy Land, especially for a younger son. He'd wanted to do his family proud, to bring them honor. The journey itself had been arduous, and Palestine had opened his eyes. A man there dared take no rest if he wanted to survive.

And then there had been Maddox DeVille. He shifted in the water and opened his eyes. There were times in life—only a few—when one met someone who gave off a light, someone so special you knew right away he would change you.

Touched by God, his *mère* used to call that sort of person. Maddox DeVille was one such. His lady, Genevieve DeClare, possibly another.

He had carried her in his heart too, right along with his promise to Maddox. Remarkable how he'd been able to see her so clearly, a picture of her painted by Maddox's adoring words. Even more remarkable how the lady in the flesh matched that picture.

Incomparable.

Pity for Maddox arose and swamped him. Because Maddox would not be able to come home to that beauteous woman. It should be Maddox here with her this Christmas.

Not me.

He took up the cloth and the pot of soap the footman had left. He scrubbed himself as if he wanted to take off the very skin. Mayhap he wanted to wash away the past along with the filth. Wash away his regret.

It was Christmas Day, and here he sat brooding. He should apply himself to elevating Mistress Genevieve's mood. If that could be done.

He climbed from the bath and dug in his pack, which the footman had left atop a chest, intending to select the least soiled of his clothing to don. The garments he'd been wearing were not there, nor were the spare items. Aghast, he stared.

Was he to remain naked?

Ah well, the footman had bade him ring if he had the

need, and this surely qualified. With haste, he wrapped the drying cloth—barely large enough for the task—around his waist, and rang for the stout footman.

****

Genevieve fought for breath as she climbed the steep stairs that led up from the kitchen to the first floor. She'd been running all morning—which, she told herself, was fortunate. Better to keep busy than have time to think.

She reflected, though, that a heavy heart did little to lighten her tasks. Things that would not have proved difficult before had now assumed daunting proportions.

The aspect of the weather, for example. And the wellbeing of her guests.

The bell from Sir Tomas's room had sounded while she was in the kitchen. Cook, in the midst of preparing the goose, just stared. One of the maids was up to her elbows in dough, and one was in the larder searching for herbs. The third had disappeared into the laundry room. As for the footmen, John was outside clearing snow and Wilfred in the hall serving their guests.

Genevieve made up her mind quickly. "I will go." Perhaps Sir Tomas had finished his bath and wanted to let them know it could now be emptied. Or perhaps he required a drink of mulled ale.

Her slippers moved over the worn stone without much sound. Tomas's door stood slightly ajar. She applied her eye and looked in.

He stood facing away from her, looking toward the window, and he was—

Mercy! Fresh out of his bath, he stood naked save for the drying cloth. She jerked away from the opening hastily, because she should not see a man, a stranger so.

Privacy was sacred, and he'd no doubt been expecting the footman.

He did not know she was there.

Holding her breath now and not making a sound, she looked again.

Oh, what a sight! His hair shone wet, tumbling in a profusion of black curls down his neck. It should have made him look feminine—but naught could be more masculine than the form on display. Broad of shoulder and well-muscled, his back tapered to a pair of lean hips and was marked by a number of scars, wounds old and new. Some of them appeared to have been applied by a lash.

In the Holy Land?

She sucked in a breath through her nose. He heard and turned around. Genevieve promptly lost all power to breathe.

In the past, she'd seen Maddox nearly naked. As children they'd gone swimming together in Father's fish pond, and both got in trouble for it. In the summer he'd often run about with his sark half open. But he'd been a boy then.

Not like this. For this was a man.

She must withdraw, had to muster some polite excuse for her presence and leave. At the very least she should avert her eyes. She could not allow herself to stand mesmerized by the glorious breadth of him, the strength in shoulders and arms. The pattern of swirling, black hair on his chest that led down, *down* and disappeared into one of her own drying cloths.

The only thing he wore.

"Mistress Genevieve?"

She averted her eyes at last, but it was too late. Heat

engulfed her, starting at her toes and flooding upward like the fires of Hell.

"I am sorry, Sir Tomas. You rang your bell." Desperate, she addressed the floor. "The footmen are otherwise engaged, so—"

Her voice failed her then. She wanted to steal another look at him. With her eyes lowered, all she could see were bare feet.

"I am devastated at troubling you, Mistress, but my clothes are all gone. I have nothing, nothing to—" His accent had thickened. Was he half as mortified as she?

"I believe they are being cleaned for you. Did Wilfred not say?"

"*Non.*"

"Wait there. I will fetch you something."

Wait there? What a foolish thing that had been to say. Where would he go, in his near-nakedness?

His near-nakedness.

She strove mightily to get her thoughts in order. As a hostess, the needs of her guests were of primary importance. Her embarrassment did not matter.

She scampered to her parents' chamber, which stood empty with Mother downstairs in company with Agnes and Uncle Gervase. She went straight to the carved chest against the wall and fell to her knees. With hasty hands, she burrowed inside. One of her father's shirts. A doublet. A pair of breeches.

Would these fit?

She thought again of what she'd seen. It seemed burned into her very brain.

With her duties as a hostess uppermost in her mind, she hurried back to Tomas's room and thrust the garments through the crack in the door.

"Here, Sir Tomas."

Not waiting for so much as a word from him, she fled.

Chapter Eight

Genevieve could not seem to rid herself of the image, that of the brawny man standing mostly naked in the firelight, nor could she dismiss the feelings the sight provoked. Even as she hurried about her duties, chased Tillie down in the laundry where the maid tried valiantly to get the dirt out of clothing little more than rags, she thought about it. About him.

She'd never known. Never known just gazing upon a man could make her feel thus. It never had before.

She understood the facts of life, to be sure. She lived on an estate that bred animals. The tenants were often plain in their speaking, and her mother had been forthright with her explanations.

What she hadn't expected were the emotions.

She liked to think of herself as sensible. Practical and levelheaded. Mayhap that was what had bothered her so much about sending Maddox away. It was out of character for her. An impulsive act of desperation.

One that had come back upon her.

Ah, well, a woman must expect to pay for her sins. If it had been wrong for her to send Maddox away—and clearly it had been, since it had cost his life—she must now endure the wages of that sin.

If the Church taught anything, it was that. No matter. Their Christmas feast was mere hours away. She would honor the holy day.

And then she would take herself away somewhere, a place where no one could see her, and weep until her eyes ran dry.

She must be a terrible sinner, though, for given the opportunity she would not be reluctant to gaze so upon Tomas Monmercy again.

****

Periods of confinement bothered Tomas and worked upon his emotions. Ever since the time spent with Maddox in their tiny hole of a cell—an age worsened only by moments of punishment and enlivened by the words they were able to share with one another—he'd found it difficult to remain shut in for long.

No air. Insufficient water. Temperatures that convinced him he would roast alive. Wormy rations. And Maddox, endlessly striving to keep his spirits up.

Would he ever escape the memories, wherever he went?

Beyond the walls of Clarendon, the storm still pounded the countryside. No matter. Driven by his restless emotions, Tomas donned his cloak over a dead man's clothes—for he had no doubt about where Mistress Genevieve had got the things he now wore—and went out.

Tiny bits of snow fell from a billowing gray sky that lowered so far it made him want to duck his head. Not a pretty snow, either, that swirled down. This came driven before an icy wind and felt like pinpricks against his skin.

The yard had been swept, the efforts of the footmen augmented by the wind, and the stones of the castle shone wet and dark.

He ducked into the stables across the way and let the

warmth find him, a scent of horses and clean hay. He must make certain his mount Algernon was being cared for. A valiant steed, Algernon, he had taken Tomas all the way to the Holy Land and back again, through dangers neither of them could have imagined.

He'd been recovered by Sir Herbert after Tomas was captured, and that good man had looked after him during Tomas's imprisonment.

So many war horses perished during the fighting, amid the dirt and blood and pain.

To his surprise, Tomas found that someone else had come to the stable before him. Not the ostler nor his young son, this figure reminded him so much of the man constantly on his mind—Maddox—that for an instant he started, then froze.

Ah, it was Maddox's young brother, Eduard. Maddox had spoken of him also, with rueful affection, since Eduard was what Maddox had called still growing into his sense of duty. The lad had now nearly achieved Maddox's height, though he still needed to fill out considerably.

He stood regarding Algernon, leaning against the stone wall opposite the big destrier's box, a brooding look on his face.

"Monsieur?" Tomas said to him inquiringly. Why would the boy be here, with Algernon?

Eduard turned guarded eyes on him. In the dim light of the stable, his hair glowed the same dull gold color as had Maddox's, back in the cell, and Tomas felt a chill of superstition.

"Is that your horse, Sir Tomas?" he asked.

"*Oui*, Master Eduard. He has been all the way to the Holy Land."

"Maddox had a horse also, a good one that he took from our estate. Dollian was one of my favorites, and was meant to be mine one day. But when Maddox decided upon the pilgrimage, Father would insist he take the best horse in the stables." Eduard's look hardened. "He took a household guard also. Three men. Did you know that?"

"I did," Tomas replied softly. "They were all killed in the melee that took place right before I met Master Maddox. He spoke of them often, while we were confined together."

"Confined. Imprisoned, you mean."

"*Oui*, Master Eduard."

For the first time, Eduard's gaze fled Tomas's. Tomas wondered if the lad had worshipped his older brother. How did he feel now, realizing the inheritance of the DeVille estate would fall to him?

"Sir Tomas, you have spoken to my parents at length, but not to me."

"I did not realize you had questions to ask, Master Eduard."

"I do." Again, Eduard's eyes came up. They were not like Maddox's in either color or expression. Throughout all Tomas had endured with him, Maddox's blue eyes had retained some blessed light.

Until the end.

Tomas spread his hands. "Ask me what you will, young master. I will do my best to answer."

Eduard's throat worked for a moment. He seemed to push the words past his lips when he spoke. "Why did you not save my brother's life? You are a great knight, are you not? A chevalier with a fine horse? He was naught but a pilgrim. Was it not your sworn task to defend him?"

Anger sounded in the lad's voice, and a great deal of condemnation. Pain filled his face. Tomas looked away from it, and studied Algernon, who looked back at him out of wise, dark eyes.

"I would that I might have done, Master Eduard. I would give much—"

The boy did not let him finish. "Then why did you not?"

"I fight with a sword. I could not use that weapon against a fever."

"You should have kept him from being captured, and from the cell where he fell ill. You, a knight."

Tomas took the accusation like the blow young Eduard meant it to be. Perhaps he should. Perhaps he could have better defended Maddox there where they'd first met, in the hot, burning light of the battle. It had been his sworn duty, as a knight.

Eduard seethed between stiff lips, "You come here and bring back that trinket—the one Genevieve gave Maddox—like some sort of hero. But I think"—he drew a breath—"I think you are nothing of the kind."

"I am no hero," Tomas agreed. He'd never claimed to be, and his own father would certainly agree with the hard assessment.

"There will be a reckoning," Eduard told him. "You just wait and see."

The lad went out then, and Tomas stood where he was, shock rippling through him. Anger, he told himself. And hurt. He could not blame Eduard for such words. The lad could not imagine what a crusader faced in the Holy Land.

He extended a hand to Algernon, trying to marshal

his thoughts well enough to follow Eduard back inside the castle. Before he could, the outer door clattered and someone came in. The ostler's young son it was. The boy came stepping up, giving Tomas an inquiring look as if he felt the discord that lingered in the air of the stable.

"He's a fine horse, Master," the boy said in awe. "Big and strong, but not mean."

"*Non*, he is never mean," Tomas agreed, reaching again to rub Algernon's nose.

"Some big horses like him are. They can fair take your head off."

"What is your name, lad?"

"Ralph, sir."

"Well, Ralph, his name's Algernon. Have you been looking after him?"

"I'm helping my father to look after him. And we live just upstairs, so it's no trouble. But there's to be a grand feast tonight, so I will be going in to the servants' hall for that."

"I am pleased to hear it."

The boy grinned. "Sir, I was wonderin'—Algernon has some marks on his hide."

"He was in the fighting, lad, in Jerusalem. Those are his scars."

Ralph's eyes grew round. "Were you in the fighting also, sir? Do you have scars too?"

Plenty of them, some that went fearfully deep.

"I thank you for looking after Algernon. And I hope you enjoy your feast."

He went back out and regarded the castle. A small fortified house, it might better be called, it had quite likely started out as a keep, probably a Saxon one. His eyes could pick out the differences in the stone. Some enterprising Norman, one called DeClare, most likely, had improved upon it, building a stout gate, a strong, square tower, and a curtain wall. Just large enough for a lord, his family, and those who served him.

What would become of the place now, with Lord William, Genevieve's father, dead? With Maddox also gone now, and no sons in the family, what would happen to it? Had Maddox made it home to wed his betrothed, it would have rested safely in that young man's hands.

Maddox would be devastated if he knew William DeClare had not survived his illness. He had been bound and determined he would offer the prayers that would make Genevieve's father well, for her sake.

Genevieve. Ah, every time Tomas so much as thought of her, everything else faded away. He saw again her expression when she'd caught him standing nearly naked, following his bath.

Had he ever seen such a look in the eyes of any woman?

She was also a woman with a broken heart, so he had better turn his thoughts away from her. She had belonged to Maddox, and her heart did still. He, Tomas, had performed a sacred duty on Maddox's behalf. No more.

No more.

He hunched his shoulders and returned to the castle.

Chapter Nine

Genevieve stood gazing around the great hall with troubled eyes. All lay in readiness for the feast, the tables set and all the candles lit. A fire roared in the enormous hearth, and she could smell the greenery that had been strewn about. The harper sat ready to play.

Why then did Genevieve feel so distraught, as if control slipped away through her very fingertips?

She walked along the table, assuring herself all had been laid correctly—as it had—and wondering.

How would she face Tomas Monmercy again?

Where to look, now that she knew some of what lay beneath his clothing?

She glanced at the harper, Master Dennis, who smiled at her. She joined him where he sat near the hearth with Rex, who seemed to have taken a liking to him, near his feet.

She'd been fortunate to hire him for the season. Such men as he wandered from place to place and were in greatest demand at this time of year.

A pleasant man, he looked to be in his late middle years, with a crop of hair just going gray and a neat beard. He half rose when Genevieve joined him. She waved him back onto his bench.

"At your ease, Master Dennis, please. I merely wanted to thank you." He had of course been present and heard what Sir Tomas had said upon his arrival. "You have been doing valiant duty, and many more hours than we agreed."

He regarded her with kindly eyes. "It is never auspicious when ill news arrives on a holy day, or the eve of one."

Genevieve nodded.

"I thought, since I am here, my music might provide some small comfort."

"And so it has. You are a most steadying presence. Please be sure to take time to feast and enjoy the holy day. You are welcome at the board with us."

"Mistress, you are kindness itself."

"Before dinner we are all going to the chapel, where my uncle will say a few words. Will you come?"

"Aye, Mistress."

The visit to the chapel proved cold and, for Genevieve at least, lent little comfort. Lady Joan and Lord Hugh did not join them then, nor did they come down for the feast. Genevieve went directly to the hall, shedding her cloak into Wilfred's hands in the entryway.

Mother entered the hall next, in company with Gilliane, followed by Agnes and her children, who immediately brought the room to life.

Mother, so Genevieve thought, did not look well, her face pinched and overly pale. Her concern, however, centered all upon Genevieve.

"My dear, can you bear up?" Mother grasped Genevieve's hands in hers.

"As needs must."

Mother's pale gray eyes met Genevieve's. "I grieve, Daughter, for your poor brave heart. I know what it is to lose the man one values above all others."

Genevieve's eyes dropped and her hands squirmed

in her mother's grasp. To be sure, Mother believed she had loved Maddox. And she had—oh, she had.

Mother hurried on. "Why, you were scarcely betrothed before he went off on his pilgrimage, on your father's behalf." Tears flooded Mother's eyes. "It is so unfair that you will never have him for husband, as was meant."

"Aye, Mother, so it is."

"Your willingness to carry on for the sake of our guests does you justice."

Genevieve ached to tell her mother—to tell someone—the truth. It seemed unworthy of the great love Maddox had held for her to pretend she had loved him in the same way.

But the rest of their guests were entering the hall, and the servants stood ready to begin carrying in the dishes. She could scarcely take her mother aside now.

Instead she said a bit vaguely, "We must bear what we are given."

Her uncle joined them. "My dear Genevieve, why do you not lead us to table? It appears all is in readiness."

Genevieve had debated, following Tomas's arrival, whether to change the seating for the feast. Her uncle, of course, sat at the head of the table with Mother on his right hand and Genevieve on his left. Tomas Monmercy, however, should have an honored place also, and so after some hesitation she'd placed him beside her.

As he approached the table, she saw he still wore her father's clothing, which only served to make her think about when she'd seen him wearing far less. He helped her to her seat, and her face warmed and she found she could not look him in the eye.

In the chapel, Genevieve had whispered several

prayers, not all of them, she feared, worthy of God's ears. For the weather to quiet. For this terrible misery on her heart to ease. For a measure of comfort with this man who had come so far to bring her the mistletoe heart.

Perhaps having him here at her side was an opportunity to find that ease.

Accordingly, she turned toward him. "I hope, Sir Tomas, you do not find us too simple in our ways here, after your far travels."

"Ah!" He smiled and tossed his head. His hair had curled most elaborately after it came clean, and ran rampant around his angular face. "What I see here is far from simple, Mistress. You have indeed provided a feast."

The table did look well with the goose at center and all the other dishes and delicacies laid out.

"Cook has worked very, very hard."

"Then we must do Cook's effort justice."

Uncle Gervase spoke a prayer. Platters were passed and presented. The children chattered about the gifts they had found upon waking that morning, in addition to what Saint Nicholas had brought them earlier in the month. Cousin Agnes's husband, Roger, spoke of affairs back in Scarborough where he managed his father's estate.

"And you, Sir Tomas," he finished. "Will you not tell us about your own lands?"

Out of the corner of her eye, Genevieve saw Tomas's hands freeze above his trencher. "Monsieur, there is not much to tell. It is a beautiful place within sight of the sea, though much more humble than this. We have been there many generations. I have three sisters, all wed and moved away, and an older brother."

Uncle Gervase nodded his understanding. "And you

did not wish to join the clergy?"

"It is not the life for me. I thought I could instead prove myself of good worth by joining the crusade to the Holy Land."

Agnes said kindly, "You will be anxious to return home after your journey of mercy here. Why, you might have been celebrating Christmas with your own family had you not brought the sad news to us, instead."

Genevieve glanced at the two empty seats at the table. Maddox's parents felt unequal to joining them, though Eduard numbered one at the table, seated opposite Gilliane.

"I do not mind, Mistress." Tomas laid aside his knife as if he no longer wanted to eat. "I understand how important Master Maddox and Mistress Genevieve were to one another."

Genevieve went warm. She could look at no one.

She was a liar. A pretender. Behaving toward everyone, especially this fine man beside her, as if she had loved Maddox with her whole heart.

Roger asked, "How long were you away from your home, Sir Tomas?"

"Two years."

"Does your family know that you are alive and well? Or will they be missing you this Christmas?"

"I do not know whether or not my commander, Sir Herbert, sent word back home. All our company, you see, are from Tregastel. He did send word home from time to time, though it is difficult to spare anyone for a messenger, and the dangers are great."

Genevieve stirred herself. "This is grim talk for a holy day." She turned to the harper. "I pray thee, Master Dennis, play us something lively when you have finished your meal."

"That I will, Mistress, and gladly."

"And," Genevieve laid her fingers lightly on the forearm of the man seated beside her, "I pray you do not let our questions put you off enjoying your own feast."

For the first time since she'd glimpsed him half naked in his chamber, their eyes met. What did she see there? A kind of humble wonderment. Oh, what a man was this!

"Mistress Genevieve, I am very glad to be here. And please know, you may ask me whatever you will."

Chapter Ten

Following the feast, Master Dennis made good on his promise and played some lively tunes, though except for the children, it did not serve to lighten the mood as much as Genevieve had hoped. She went upstairs to make sure Maddox's parents had received the meals she had sent up, and had all they needed.

"My wife is prostrate," Lord Hugh told her at the door of their chamber. "We will leave for home just as soon as the weather permits."

"I shall be sorry to see you go." They were, just like Maddox, a part of her life from as far back as she could remember. A last tie with Maddox that she hoped would not break.

"Perhaps a word from you will persuade Lady Joan to stay."

Lady Joan lay upon the bed, looking small and terribly frail. Genevieve tiptoed forward, brushed aside the bed hangings, and sat on the edge of the mattress.

"Oh, Genevieve!" Lady Joan exclaimed, and reached for her hand. "My dear, you are the only one who can possibly understand our loss, since you share it."

Ready tears flowed from Lady Joan's eyes. This woman had always carried a quiet joy, and had a smile of sweetness that rivaled Maddox's. Now gone, all gone.

Lord Hugh said, "Sir Tomas has agreed to speak with us at length before we go, here in the privacy of our chamber, and tell us more of Maddox's last moments. Sir Tomas was with him all the while."

"How very kind of him." And how difficult that would have to be.

"I need to know my son was at peace when he left this earthly realm. So far—so far from home."

"He was a son of whom any father would be proud." Lord Hugh looked grave. "And we were always proud of him. Every day of his life. But for him to take on such a brave, sacred duty at the end—there are no words."

Genevieve hoped they did not blame her, these good, decent people, for costing Maddox his life. God knew, Gilliane did, as if Genevieve did not blame herself enough.

Lady Joan gripped Genevieve's fingers still more tightly. "I hope—I hope you can forgive Maddox, my dear."

"Forgive?" She, to forgive him?

"For failing to offer the prayers that might have saved your dear father's life."

Hot tears stung Genevieve's eyes. "I blame Maddox for nothing."

"Perhaps…perhaps Sir Tomas can tell you more of Maddox's last moments also. Mayhap 'twill bring you comfort."

If anything could. Guilt lay in a hard ball in Genevieve's gut.

"If only," Lord Hugh mused, "we could have brought the lad home, home to lie with his ancestors where he belongs. It wounds me to think of him forever in that foreign land of sand and blood and—and death."

"His spirit is not there," Genevieve assured him. "It cannot linger in that foreign place. It is here, with you."

"It is in Heaven, where he belongs," Lady Joan insisted. "Or if anywhere, it would be here with you, dear Genevieve. He loved you so deeply."

The tears flowed unstinted down Genevieve's cheeks.

"We will take our opportunity to speak with Tomas tomorrow morning, and then hopefully make our way home," said Lord Hugh.

Genevieve nodded and arose. She wanted to say so much more, wanted to tell them Maddox would not want them to grieve so terribly for him, would not wish to witness their heartbreak.

But who was she to give such advice? She, who had caused their misery.

****

By the time Genevieve returned to the hall, Agnes had taken the children—worn out by the excitement of receiving their gifts and by being permitted to join the feast—up to bed. The harper had gone off to the servants' hall to provide music for their festivities, which would go late into the night. Genevieve would have to be careful not to call upon any of them too early on the morrow.

Gilliane and Eduard, rather surprisingly, spoke softly together. She found her mother, Uncle Gervase, and Sir Tomas sitting at the table, speaking most earnestly.

"Come, Daughter, sit." Mother held out a hand to Genevieve. "Sir Tomas was just telling us of the Holy Land."

Genevieve sat beside her mother, which put her opposite Sir Tomas. He raised his eloquent, dark eyes to her and gave her a look she could not interpret.

Uncle Gervase, who had been a knight in his younger days, shook his head with a gleam of admiration in his eyes.

"I always wanted to make the pilgrimage, in days gone. I feel the best of us are called upon to do so. But I had responsibilities here in England that I could not forsake."

Sir Tomas nodded soberly. "I thought I was prepared for what I would find in Jerusalem. I had heard tales from those who went before me. Nothing, though, could prepare a man."

He and Uncle Gervase spoke on for a while about the necessities of such a journey. The supplies. The horses.

"One thing I did not expect," Tomas confessed, "was the rampant illness that runs riot in the Holy Land and, indeed, all along the route. Nor was I prepared for the heat. We have nothing like to it, in Brittany."

"Or indeed, here in England, I will warrant."

"It is difficult to escape the heat for even a brief span of time. The nights are cooler, but not enough to provide real relief. I have seen men drowning in sweat and those who, trapped in their armor, received burns from the inside out."

Eduard and Gilliane, at the other end of the table, now listened.

Mother exclaimed, "It troubles me to think of Maddox in such a place, a place without mercy!" She looked at Genevieve. "I regret, oh, how I regret ever having sent him."

You did not, Genevieve wanted to say. It was my doing. But she sat with her hands folded and her eyes lowered, even as Rex came and laid his great head in her lap.

At last Uncle Gervase rose from his place. "Well, Sister, I am ready for my bed. Genevieve, thank you for your efforts to provide a merry Christmas for us all." His kindly gray eyes captured hers. "It cannot have been easy for you."

"Uncle, you are most welcome."

"Gervase, I will go up with you. And you, Gilliane, come along. Genevieve, dear, do not stay up too long."

They went out, and after stealing a look or two at Sir Tomas, Eduard followed them. Genevieve sat where she was, not daring to meet the gaze of the man opposite her. She gazed at the table instead and at his hands that rested upon it. Beautiful hands, despite the scars, broad in the palms, and strong.

"Mistress Genevieve," his soft voice broke the quiet of the hall, "I wanted to say I hope I did not spoil your Christmas celebration. To bring such news at a joyous time. I confess I did not think. I thought only of fulfilling the promise I made to Maddox."

"Sir Tomas, I needed to know the truth, difficult as it was to hear. To be frank with you, I half expected Maddox to be here in time for Christmas. Then it would have been a true celebration. 'Tis why I wanted his family here. How wonderful it would have been, if he'd come walking in—" Her throat closed.

"*Oui*, so it would."

"My expectations, born of my own hope, are not your responsibility. There is no fault to you. You have acted with honor in fulfilling your promise."

"He wanted so much for you to have the return of the mistletoe heart. He carried it inside his shirt, close against his heart. I hope you do not mind, but on my way to you I did the same, wore it close where I knew it was safe."

Her eyes rose to meet his at last. What did she see there? The same devotion she'd beheld when he'd arrived. When he'd thrown himself at her feet. Along with what might be admiration and a touch of wry understanding.

He shrugged. "It seemed the only place for something so precious."

Precious. Against his heart. What a valiant, steadfast heart it must be.

"I appreciate the measures you have taken, Sir Tomas, and the trouble to which you have gone."

"*Ce n'est rien*, I assure you. As soon as the weather clears, I will depart for home and intrude no further upon you."

"Pray, Sir Tomas, do not hurry yourself on my account."

Chapter Eleven

Tomas arose early the next morning, stopped by the chapel to say his prayers, and headed for the stable.

The prayers, so he feared, were in this case a matter of rote. He had spouted so many prayers while in the Holy Land he was no longer convinced God listened. During his imprisonment, and directly after, his prayers had started out as a comfort, only to become a frustration to him.

A man could not pray any harder than he had when Maddox, who had become so dear to him, lay dying. He'd even asked God to take him, Tomas, instead of Maddox, so Maddox could return home to his love.

Who was he, after all, but an insignificant second son? Whereas Maddox was cherished by his parents. And by his betrothed, Genevieve.

He recalled how she'd looked sitting across from him at the table last evening, the firelight warming her flawless skin, her lips the color of sweet roses. And those eyes, that so clearly revealed her emotions.

Oui, Maddox had described her well. His betrothed. His beloved. Incomparable.

He found the stables deserted when he arrived. He'd anticipated it would be so. The servants' celebrations had continued late last night. It was only to be expected they would not be astir early.

He did not mind the solitude, shared with the horses.

It reminded him of being at home, where he'd often helped care for his father's animals.

He found Algernon munching contentedly on the remnants of yesterday's hay, gave him a good grooming, and checked the wounds the horse had collected during their journey across Europe. After, he checked on the other beasts and, taking up a broom, swept out the place from end to end.

He was sweeping the snow from outside the door when the ostler and his young son, Ralph, came down from their quarters.

The ostler looked startled to see him. "Master? What be ye about?"

"Just enjoying the quiet morning."

"My lord, ye should not be doing my job for me."

Tomas handed over the broom. "Why not?" He smiled. "You are taking good care of my mount and I am grateful."

"Aye, sir."

Genevieve treated her servants well, as Tomas had already noted. He liked that. Why should he not do the same?

"I have given them all new feed."

"Sir, I thank ye."

The ostler and his son went inside, while Tomas remained out in the morning. The wind had died, though it continued cold and wet. As he crossed the yard, pellets of icy snow struck his face and found their way down his neck.

When would it be possible for him to travel? Genevieve had invited him to stay for the rest of the holy season. And he believed she meant it, but perhaps it would be better for her if he left—let her have her mourning without him there as a constant reminder of what she'd lost.

As if she needed a reminder. Poor maiden. To lose her father, and her beloved so soon after.

Oui, he needed to leave as soon as he could. First, however, he had to give her and Maddox's young brother, Eduard, whatever answers they might seek from him. Answers to the questions that haunted a person went far to provide peace to an aching heart.

In the hall, he found the harper already astir and taking breakfast with Genevieve's uncle and mother. Despite last night's festivities in the servants' hall, the cook had arisen early enough to prepare the repast.

Lord Gervase hailed him. "Sir Tomas, come and join us. Have you been outside? How do you find the weather?"

Tomas joined them at the board, bowing to Genevieve's mother, Lady Maude. The woman had the same pale gray eyes as Genevieve, and gave him a similarly sweet smile.

"Somewhat improved, my lord, though I fear not yet ready for travel."

"Well," said Lady Maude, "I suppose that means Lord Hugh and Lady Joan will not be able to leave as they wished. At least we are all safe and warm here together, and can endure the storm. Pity the poor travelers who were caught out."

Lady Agnes came in, both her children scampering ahead of her. At the ages of six and eight, as Tomas would guess, the younglings had far too much energy to be trapped indoors for so long. Lady Agnes wore a pained look.

"Roger will be right down. Aunt Maude, I am not

sure how long we can stay. Roger is worried about the state of things at home."

"Surely you will stay till Three Kings Day!"

"I am not certain. With the children running riot—"

"But we get to see you so seldom."

"If you would permit," Tomas spoke, "I have promised to speak with Lord Hugh and Lady Joan this morn. Until they arise, you could allow me to teach the young ones the game of Alquerque. I encountered it in the Holy Land and have a cloth and markers in my pack. It may while away many hours."

"Oh, that is kind, Sir Tomas. If you have the patience for it and would not mind?"

"I do not mind."

He rose to go and fetch the game cloth. At the entry to the hall, he encountered Mistress Genevieve on her way in.

She paused and her eyes met his. "Sir Tomas, good morn. I trust you slept well."

He had not. Dreams had troubled him as they so often did, prompting raw emotions. The latter included some he did not think he should own, and they all sprang to life upon seeing her again.

She smelled of lavender, even here in the midst of winter. She looked delicate, graceful, and lovely, her head barely topping his shoulder. The color came and went in her face, kindling the radiance of which Maddox had so often spoken.

Tomas, you should see her. The beauty of her glorious features aside, she glows with an inner light.

Tomas saw that now for himself, and it touched him on a level that shook him. A woman in a thousand was Genevieve DeClare.

She held him with her gaze, and he could not look away. For several moments they connected with one another, eye to eye, spirit to spirit, before he bowed his head, whispered something—he did not know what—and slipped out of the hall.

He could feel her regard as she gazed after him, clear as the touch of her hand.

****

The game of Alquerque proved popular with not only the children but Eduard and Gilliane as well. Even the adults joined in. Lord Gervase, to be sure, already knew how to play, though he claimed he had not done so in some time. They sat around the big table to take instruction, and quiet laughter ensued.

It was, Tomas thought, like being with family, though these could scarcely be less like his own folk. His father wore his authority like a cloak, and his mother proved always obedient. He had been close to his sisters for a time, but they had left to marry early and now had families of their own.

The warmth amid which he now found himself charmed him. Maddox's parents, of course, did not come down, and Sir Hugh sent a message via Eduard, saying Lady Joan was feeling too low to meet with Tomas, and they would not be attempting to travel today.

Eduard's demeanor remained dour and glum. Despite that, Tomas felt at ease in a way he had not in a long time.

It pleased him to laugh again and to make others laugh. Tomas had striven mightily to lighten Maddox's moods during their imprisonment together, and through the sharing of nonsense had even surprised a laugh or two from him during those endless hours, the days upon days to get through, all overshadowed by the threat of what was to come. For Maddox's amusement, Tomas had spun the many stories taught to him in his youth, of beautiful damsels and knights sworn to honor them. Maddox had spoken of his own damsel, with tender eagerness.

She'd seemed like another story then, a dream. Difficult to believe Tomas sat here now with that very lady across the table where he could watch the laughter come and go in her face.

When their hands nearly met as they reached for a game marker, she became all too real, just like the emotions she inspired.

Sitting there as the afternoon passed, he understood. He saw why Maddox had adored her, idolized her, and raised her so high in his estimation. He comprehended why that young man had undertaken an arduous quest, to take her prayers for her father to Jerusalem.

This warmth Tomas now experienced should be Maddox's, not his. As should Genevieve's smile, and the laughter in her eyes. For her sake, Tomas wished it could be so.

Chapter Twelve

Early the next morning, Tomas was astir and back out to the stables sweeping the boxes, where the ostler once more caught him. The man, called Roderick, protested.

"Master, I cannot let ye be doing the lad's work, nor mine."

"It is good for me. I wish to be useful." During his imprisonment, Tomas had wanted nothing more than to be at liberty to do some work, to use his muscles. "My father taught me no job on the estate is below its master. Besides, Algernon likes for me to care for him."

The stableman still looked shocked, but young Ralph, who accompanied his father, grinned. He it was who helped Tomas sweep the yard after, out toward the entrance way.

The storm itself appeared to have passed, but the aftermath still held the countryside in its grip. Heavy clouds hung overhead, above the deep chill of true winter. As Tomas saw when he went to survey it, the road remained impassable, an unbroken expanse of snow topped with ice from hedgerow to hedgerow.

He was still contemplating it when Mistress Genevieve joined him, all wrapped in her cloak of blue wool. Her cheeks bloomed with rose from the cold, and her lips were the deep red of berries.

"Good morn," she bid him, a measure of hesitance

in her eyes. "Roderick has informed me you helped sweep out the yard. There is no need, you know."

"I wished—needed—to do something useful."

She nodded as if she understood.

He gazed once more at the road. "It does not appear as if Maddox's family will be able to leave today, either."

"Nay, it is a dismal aspect. I feel so bad for them. I fear for Lady Joan's health, with her so low yesterday, and especially after they return home. I worry she may pine and languish."

"It helps to have a purpose, so I do believe."

"Aye. Sir Tomas?" She turned her eyes on him. "And what is your purpose to be?"

A goodly question. His sole thought up till now had been of returning to her the mistletoe heart. He had done service in the Holy Land, and presumably proved his worth to his father, so he could return home. But what work to take up there?

"I am not certain," he admitted. "While in Saladin's prison, I thought only of achieving freedom, as a purpose. Now I have none."

"Then, for a time, allow freedom to be your guiding star." She started walking back to the castle and he fell in beside her, only to pause when she did.

"How beautiful it looks," she observed, "with snow decorating it from top to bottom, and the green boughs above the door. Maddox would have been master here, given my father's death—that is what Father wanted. He was ever so fond of Maddox."

"What will happen now?"

"My uncle will oversee the running of the estate until other plans are made. He has promised Mother's security, and mine, are assured." Her words sounded brave but a grim expression invaded her eyes.

"Other plans?"

She glanced at him. "I will be expected to marry. The estate will pass to my husband."

A pain started at Tomas's heart. She belonged to Maddox. How could she wed another?

"I wish," he murmured, "I wish that Maddox, rather than I, had been the one to return. Return to you."

She swiveled to face him. "Do not say such a thing. It is a sin."

"It is the truth. I should have been the one to take the fever, in that prison. Then you would have had the one you love here with you. You would have been happy."

She reached for his hand. Fragile as her fingers felt, they gripped his tightly.

"Sir Tomas, 'tis not up to us who should live and who should die. It is the will of God."

"If I could have died in his place, I would have."

"Then you were—and are—a good friend to him. I am glad he had you there at the end." Once more, her eyes sought his. "And I am glad to have you here now, with me."

If only. If only he could make her truly glad.

"Come, Sir Tomas, let us go to our breakfast. You have most certainly earned it."

****

After breakfast, Hugh DeVille and his son, Eduard, went out in turn and inspected the road. He came back shaking his head.

"It seems, my dear Lady Maude," he said to Mother, "we will have to impose upon you a while longer."

"My good man, it is not an imposition. Do you think you might persuade Lady Joan to come down from her chamber? I would love her company."

"I do not know whether she feels equal to it."

"Then I will go up and spend the morning with her, if she will welcome me."

"I am sure she would enjoy that."

In the afternoon, the youngsters went out to play in the snow. When Genevieve walked out a while later to see how they fared, she found them playing with the stable boy and his little sister, along with the cook's young son and Sir Tomas. The children, it seemed, were not the only ones with energy to burn.

The six of them made snowballs which they tossed at one another, ducked and dove, the children giggling. Sir Tomas's dark eyes danced with laughter.

When he caught sight of Genevieve, however, he sobered.

"Forgive me, Mistress Genevieve. I did not mean to make so light during a time of mourning."

She glanced at Eduard, who stood with his hands clasped behind his back, next to—of all people—Gilliane. Neither of them had joined in but watched the play. "Nonsense. The children need the relief, as do we all."

Maddox definitely had not been the man to condemn laughter. Indeed, when Genevieve looked back upon their many days together, whether sunlit or otherwise, it was the laughter she remembered most of all.

She and Tomas walked inside together, leaving the youngsters capering. He said, "Mistress Genevieve, I have to admit, I admire the way you conduct your household. You stand not on ceremony with your guests, and treat your servants as family."

"'Tis as my father always did. He saw no need to be

harsh with those who answered to him."

"That cannot be said of many men." Tomas wrinkled his brow. "Those I have met, save Sir Herbert, perhaps, who is of good and generous spirit, seem to think they can and must impose measures of control."

Genevieve stole a look at him. Did he refer to his own father?

"We are a small household here. And Father loved to hear others laugh."

She paused inside the doorway to remove her cloak.

"A remarkable man indeed. It will be difficult for you to reconcile losing him."

"To be truthful with you, Sir Tomas, I am not certain I can. He loved the Christmas season, which is why I determined to hold these festivities this year, even though we are in mourning. I hoped it might lift Mother's spirits."

Tomas found her eyes and engaged them. "And here am I, bringing you still more grief."

"None of it seems real. I keep expecting Father to come down those stairs, all excited for our visitors, and to find Maddox at the gate. To walk into the next room and discover them talking together."

He reached out and took her hands. His fingers cradled her chilly ones, and lent warmth. "I would that I could take the burden of your grief onto my own heart."

"You have, Sir Tomas, in great measure. Just having you here eases my sadness." Indeed it was true, in ways she did not understand and so could not explain to him.

Gilliane came in then, pushing past them where they stood close together in the rear entry. She cast a searing look at Genevieve before dropping her gaze to where Sir Tomas gripped her hands. Swiftly, Genevieve pulled her fingers away.

She had done nothing wrong. Why should she allow her sister's sharp look to make her feel she had? As if she had betrayed Maddox somehow...

Because, in truth she had. Oh, she had.

Chapter Thirteen

Genevieve tiptoed into the solar, where she'd followed her sister after removing her cloak. She found Gilliane poking the fire angrily and with unaccustomed force, causing the sparks to fly up from the wood and endangering her own clothing.

"Gilliane?"

Gilliane spun. When she saw Genevieve, her expression hardened, though Genevieve thought she'd caught a glimpse of tears in her sister's eyes.

"What do you want?"

"To speak with you, only." The solar lay empty save for the two of them. As good a time as any to try and speak again with her sister—though nothing in Gilliane's demeanor appeared welcoming.

"I have no wish to speak with you." Gilliane sniffed. "In truth, I know not who you are, any more."

"Your sister, still," Genevieve said slowly, and Gilliane shot her an even more resentful look.

"I do not think so. My sister would not do what you have done."

"What have I done?" Genevieve asked, though her heart began beating double time. It seemed almost as if Gilliane were her conscience, with a self-denouncement she did not want to face.

For an instant, she did not think her sister would reply. Then, hands clenched into fists, Gilliane swung to face her. "Do you not miss him? Do you not mourn him at all?"

"Maddox?" Genevieve's breath went tight in her chest. "Of course I do."

"Well, you do not behave like it! I have seen you shed few tears for him—"

"I have shed them, Gilliane. When I am alone, mostly."

"If you'd loved him, truly loved him, you would not be able to keep from weeping, night and day."

"Believe me, and truly, sister, I grieve for Maddox. More than you can know."

"Then why is it you look at Sir Tomas as you do?"

"What?"

"I have seen you," Gilliane lowered her voice to a vicious throb, even though there was no one else to hear. "Admiring him. Looking at him as if he, and not Maddox, were your love."

"That is a grievous thing to say. And untrue."

Gilliane sneered, "You do not lie well, sister."

Genevieve groped for a way to defuse her sister's anger, and reason through the accusation. "You mistake my welcome to Sir Tomas. He is our guest. I seek only to make certain he feels at ease here among us."

"Oh, and you do a wondrous job! I do not doubt he feels welcome."

"Gilliane, come and sit down with me. Let us discuss the matter."

"What is there to discuss? You find much to admire in Sir Tomas. Far more than in Maddox, perhaps?"

Genevieve's cheeks flamed. "Gilliane, Sir Tomas did us a very great service, bringing word—"

"Eduard says 'tis Sir Tomas's fault that Maddox is

dead."

"What!"

"He says that if Sir Tomas were half the great knight he pretends, he would have defended Maddox. Neither of them would ever have been taken prisoner. Maddox—Maddox would yet be alive!"

"Hush! Keep your voice down, pray. Since when do you listen to aught Eduard says?" From time out of mind, the two of them had detested one another. Maddox used to joke about it, how it was fortunate that he and Genevieve cared for each other so deeply, or the two estates would never have any hope of being joined. She remembered Gilliane throwing windfall apples at Eduard, and calling him the most unpleasant young man in Christendom.

As he could often be, Genevieve acknowledged. Just as Gilliane could be headstrong and difficult. Like now.

"Since he has begun to talk sense," Gilliane retorted. "None of this had to happen. You did not have to send Maddox away. He did not have to be captured, if he had such a stout knight there to defend him. Maddox did not have to die."

Suddenly, Gilliane was sobbing, with her tears overflowing and streaming in ugly tracks down her cheeks. Genevieve caught her hands.

"Come, sit down," she said again, and drew her sister to the bench.

As soon as she was seated, Gilliane drew her hands from Genevieve's, as if she could not bear the touch. It felt like a slap across the face.

"I understand, Gilliane," Genevieve said slowly, "that you had fond feelings for Maddox. Like a brother, perhaps."

Gilliane lowered her hands and glared at Genevieve. "Not like a brother! Why do you assume that because I am young my love for him was not genuine? I am nearly of an age to wed. He did not want me." Now rage stared from Gilliane's eyes. "He wanted you. I cannot imagine why, when you valued him so little that you would send him away without a thought."

Because he did not know I valued him so little, Genevieve thought, and grief swamped her, so deep and paralyzing she could not think beyond it. Gilliane was right. She had not deserved Maddox's love.

She fought to speak. "Gilliane, Maddox was very, very dear to me, and I loved him a great deal."

"Then why? You just found out he is dead, and you are looking at another man."

I must be more careful, Genevieve thought. And indeed, it may be best if Sir Tomas leaves as soon as ever he can. Because I cannot control the way I look upon him, or control how I feel when I do. "Sister," she began.

Gilliane surged to her feet. "I will not sit here and listen to your excuses. If you had loved Maddox as I— as you should, you would never have sent him away."

"Father—"

"Nay, not even for Father."

Genevieve bowed her head.

Gilliane hissed, "Your selfishness caused his death. And I will never, never forgive you."

She ran out, the way a girl half her age might, her slippers slapping on the stone floor. Outside the windows the wind was rising, snarling like an angry beast, tearing around the stones.

Genevieve sat where she was, in a position of mourning. Gilliane would never forgive her, nay. How could she, then, ever hope to forgive herself?

Chapter Fourteen

The air was still and felt very cold as Tomas entered the little stone chapel the next morning. He'd risen from a bed in which he'd found little sleep, with a troubled mind. He needed to order his thoughts before he encountered anyone, most particularly Mistress Genevieve.

The interior of the chapel held the chill of death, and the cold bit at his exposed skin. His breath came in small, foggy bursts as he walked down the center aisle to face the altar.

Figures lay to either side of him, in eternal sleep— Genevieve's ancestors. The stone effigy of a knight in full armor to his left and along the other wall another such, with his lady.

Was Genevieve's father laid here also?

He knelt upon the stone and lifted his eyes to the small rose window above the chancel. He'd come here to pray. He found himself wishing he could talk to Maddox, instead.

Talking to Maddox had been so easy. They had spent untold hours at it, and there had been few thoughts they could not express or exchange.

Hard to believe they had not known each other when they'd been thrown into the cell together. Just two young men, one from the north of England and one from the north of France. They had little in common save perhaps a similarity in rank.

Maddox had a loving family, a father who adored him. His future was assured, the inheritance of his father's estate and its increase through marriage. Not just any marriage, either, but one to a woman he prized above all others.

Tomas—well, *oui*, he had the affection of his mother and his sisters, but he was an afterthought to his father. Would his father even care if he failed to come home?

From the very first, Tomas had envied Maddox a little and half wished they could have traded places. An unworthy thought, with the way things had turned out. And now—now—with the way he felt...

"Forgive me, my friend." He spoke to Maddox rather than to God, after all. "I think I am falling in love with your Genevieve."

He had a sudden vision of Maddox's blue eyes gazing at him from out of a thin, wasted face, one battered and bruised from the latest beatings. Kindness rested in those eyes, a kindness that never wavered no matter what they endured.

Tomas, how could you do anything other than love her?

Tomas bowed his head on a sudden rush of pain.

Did I not tell you she is incomparable?

"*Oui*. She is just as you described. Warm. Generous. Beautiful. I listened to all your tales of her, and I must confess, I thought them colored by the workings of your heart. When a man loves so, I told myself, there does he behold perfection. And by all the saints, you did love her."

Aye I did. I do.

"Me, I will admit to you now, my friend, I envied you a little. I did not understand what it meant to be in love."

A short silence met these words, the space of ten heartbeats.

And do you understand it now, Tomas, what it means to love?

"I cannot. I dare not. She is yours."

Maddox—or more precisely, his spirit—said nothing.

"The guilt I feel is—is more than I can express. But even that will not change my feelings toward her. I cannot sleep for these feelings, for longing to see her and be in her company. For the sound of her voice, her laughter."

Her laughter is a song.

"So you did say. I failed to understand. Tell me, my friend, you who at so many dark moments told me how to go on, what may I do with these feelings?"

Ah, we shared much when we endured together, did we not? In our darkest moments.

"So we did."

You helped me through many a desperate time, telling me when I doubted it most that I would see her again. You brought to her the symbol of my promise, my love.

I say to you, Tomas, if you love her, lose no guilt in it. You are alive to love as I am not.

The generosity of it stole Tomas's breath. The guilt he felt, however, was not so easily defeated. He bowed his head and whispered, "Forgive me."

When he again lifted his head, all traces of Maddox had gone. He was alone in the frigid chapel, save for the sleeping dead.

****

"I suppose you think you are clever."

The voice sounded so much like Maddox's—like what Tomas had just heard in the chapel—it spun him around on his heels. Indeed, at first glance, the figure facing him looked like Maddox's also, though bundled mightily against the cold, as Tomas had never seen him. The same height. The same gleam of dark-gold hair.

Tomas gasped, "I beg your pardon?"

The figure took a step closer, and Tomas knew him. Not Maddox, but his young brother.

Eduard glared into Tomas's face, his features twisted in the clear morning light. Anger shone there, and a measure of spite that should at once have told Tomas this could not be Maddox.

"*Monsieur* Eduard. Do you take exception to me?"

"I do! Most assuredly, Sir Tomas, I do. You come here playing at the innocent, expressing your grief on our behalf. But what grief could you feel at my brother's loss, when you barely knew him?"

"I did know your brother, *Monsieur* Eduard. I knew him very well."

"For how long? A few weeks? A month?"

How could Tomas explain to this young lad, safe in the grasp of his family, that intimacy was not always measured in time, but in experience?

"During that short time, we shared much."

Eduard's head jerked up. "I am surprised you have the temerity to come here at all."

"Why is that? I came to keep a promise to your brother, to return—"

"The trinket, aye, so you said. Or perhaps it was to

worm your way into his place? When all the while 'tis your fault he is dead."

"My fault?" Not that, again.

"Aye, you the grand knight with the destrier and all the other grand trappings. As I say, if you were half the knight you claim to be, you would have defended him, there in Jerusalem, and kept him from being captured in the first place."

Tomas bowed his head. "It is true. It was my duty to protect all pilgrims and those who followed the cross—"

"So you admit your perfidy!"

"*Monsieur* Eduard, I understand that your grief—your grief makes you want to place blame. If you could have seen the circumstances there that day, you would know that no man could have prevented what happened." Though he had thought about it, had he not? Gone over and over the circumstances of that last battle. It had not even been a battle so much as a skirmish that had got out of hand, with Saracens on all sides, and a mob of pilgrims that had included Maddox and his household guard, in the way.

The guard had fallen quickly. And how Maddox had later mourned the loss of those brave men.

This boy could not imagine it. Tomas could not try to make him understand.

"You are a coward and a fraud," Eduard declared angrily. "And a trickster for coming here and making everyone believe your tales. It should have been my brother walking in through that door." The anger in his voice had turned to hate.

"*Oui, monsieur,*" Tomas agreed. "So it should."

"You admit it then? You admit your perfidy!"

"I would have died for Maddox. I would have perished, if it would have sent him home."

Eduard leaned toward him, his eyes glowing blue in the growing light. A sneer twisted his young lips. "Then why, Sir Tomas, is he not here?"

Not giving Tomas a chance to answer, Eduard stalked away from him. He would challenge me, if he were older, Tomas thought. He would slay me, if he could.

There was but one thing to be done. He must withdraw as swiftly as possible from this situation. And until then, he must keep himself to himself and remember, always remember, all that lay here belonged to Maddox, and not to him.

Chapter Fifteen

"Mother, I fear somewhat is amiss with Sir Tomas. Can you fathom it?"

Lady Maude turned her head when Genevieve spoke, and looked askance. They were alone in the solar, Gilliane being closeted her own room, Agnes busy with the children, and Maddox's mother once more confined to her chamber.

"What makes you say something is amiss with him?"

"I am not certain." Genevieve wagged her shoulders uneasily. "All was fine with him yesterday afternoon when we met outside, while the children were playing. Today he has barely spared a word"—or indeed, a look—"for me."

"Perhaps he grows tired of our company. We are after all a sad little group, likely too dull for him."

"Mayhap." But Genevieve did not think it was that. Her every instinct told her that Tomas avoided her company in particular.

But why?

"I thought I saw him headed outside earlier," Mother said.

"Again?" Genevieve crossed to the window. "It grows dark so early at this time of year. And," she fretted, "it has once more begun snowing. Why would he remain outside?"

"Who can tell? It has been a dreadful winter so far. And so much of it yet to be endured. You know, Genevieve, when you first suggested keeping the holiday this year, I was uncertain. But now I feel it was entirely the right thing to do. Your father always hated it when we fell into low spirits. We should make the most of what time we have left together before Master Dennis, the harper, leaves. I think we should have music this evening, and dancing."

"Do you?"

"Most assuredly. Our guests have traveled far to be with us. And your dear father would not wish us to wallow in grief."

"Aye, Mother, no doubt you are right. I will just go down and speak to Master Dennis."

And perhaps watch for Sir Tomas to put in an appearance.

Genevieve found Uncle Gervase in the hall with the harper, sharing a game of Alquerque. They employed the cloth Tomas had left there, and sat at their ease. Uncle Gervase looked up at Genevieve with a welcoming smile.

"Master Dennis was just telling me tales of his many journeyings. The places he and his harp have been put my old travels as a knight to shame."

"I can only imagine." Genevieve seated herself beside her uncle. "Master Dennis, where have you been?"

"Well, to Ireland where I learned many of my tunes. That was in my youth, of course. To Wales where I enhanced them." Again he smiled. "And even to France a time or two."

To Brittany? Genevieve wondered. She had spent

her whole life here at Clarendon. She could scarcely imagine the land from which Sir Tomas had come. Nor could she truly fathom the distance to the Holy Land.

She should have considered that distance before she sent Maddox so far.

"Dare I ask, Master Dennis, which country you like best?"

"Ah, Mistress Genevieve, that is a difficult question. There is magic everywhere. But I was born near York and find myself returned here now that I am aging. I suppose everyone comes home, in the end."

Aye, but what was home? A physical dwelling place, or a spiritual one?

She told him, "The magic you have gathered sounds in your music. We are fortunate indeed to have you here for the season."

He bowed his head.

"I wondered if we might impose upon your good nature a bit farther this evening? Mother has suggested dancing."

"Your mother has?" Uncle Gervase lifted his brows.

"Aye. She wishes to provide our guests what pleasure we can."

Master Dennis gave her a kindly look. "I live to play, Mistress Genevieve."

"I am sure," Uncle Gervase told the harper, "you are used to playing for much larger companies."

They chatted on while they finished their game, and Genevieve let her gaze drift toward the door. What if Sir Tomas had departed? What if despite the foul weather he'd decided he could no longer stay?

He owed them nothing beyond what he'd already given.

But surely, surely he would not leave without saying a word? A gentleman would not do so, nor would a friend. And what grew between them—for something most assuredly did—must at the very least go by the name of friendship.

She thought of him outside in the stable yard, lobbing snowballs at the children, and of the smile in his eyes when he looked at her. Friendship, aye.

If Maddox had valued him as a friend, could she do otherwise? Only—only 'twas not merely friendship she felt.

She got to her feet so abruptly, she startled the two men playing at their game.

"Forgive me," she murmured. "I must away to the kitchen and make sure all is in readiness for our meal."

"Aye, my dear." Uncle Gervase gave her a puzzled look. "As you will."

The kitchen lacked the chaotic energy it had achieved on Christmas Day. Cook hummed to herself as she worked at the big table, and her maids held their accustomed posts. They had fallen into a comfortable rhythm while caring for their guests.

Genevieve discussed the courses with Cook and glanced at the door. "Are you lacking in anything?"

"Nay, Mistress. As you can see, I have the pies all ready. And the syllabub."

"Has—has anyone seen Sir Tomas this afternoon?"

Cook looked surprised, and the nearest kitchen maid jerked her head around.

"Mercy, Mistress Genevieve, I've not been away from my pots all the day long."

Genevieve's cheeks flamed. She made a fool of herself over this. Yet—perhaps she had time before supper to look outside.

She was about to go fetch her cloak when a commotion sounded at the door. Wilfred, the footman, entered in company with Sir Tomas, each of them toting a load of firewood.

Genevieve's relief at seeing Sir Tomas fair staggered her. He came in from the gathering dark with his head bare and snowflakes shining on the black locks, conversing with Wilfred as if they were old companions. A check interrupted his step when he saw Genevieve, and his expression sobered.

"Mistress? Is something gone amiss?"

"Sir Tomas, you need not help with the chores while you are our guest."

He shrugged, even as Wilfred moved off with his load.

"Your man looked to be burdened down, and I do not mind. It is better, I find, to keep busy, as it quells the—the troubling thoughts in my mind."

Genevieve nodded and stepped closer. She sought his gaze and lowered her voice. "I wondered whether—and feared—you had gone. Gone from here without a word."

He froze where he stood. She could smell the cold coming off him, and see a drop or two of melted snow hanging from his long lashes.

"Mistress Genevieve, I would not do that, leave—leave you without a word."

Her gaze clung to his. "Do I have your promise on that?" A promise, as she well knew, meant much to this man, and she had no right to ask for one. But the thought that he could go, ride out of her life so that she might never see him again, frightened her so. She must ask.

His tight expression softened. She saw warmth flood his eyes, and kindness. So much kindness. A fathomless strength.

"I do so promise. I will not leave without thanking you properly for your hospitality."

Fine, that. Except she did not want him to leave at all. Mayhap if he came to her first, she could dissuade him from any such departure.

"Meanwhile…" He summoned up a smile. "Please allow me to perform what services I may. We are a small household, and as I say, I much prefer being employed."

"As you wish." She would grant him whatever he requested, whatever pleased him. "Now do come and get warm. Supper will be sent in soon."

He carried his load of wood to the hall as if he'd done so a score of other times, as if he belonged there with them. Genevieve followed him, wondering at the simple contentment that lodged in her breast.

****

Something in Mistress Genevieve's demeanor had changed. Tomas could feel that. Since he'd helped Wilfred carry in their load of firewood, she had unquestionably warmed toward him. All through the meal, whenever he glanced up, he encountered her eyes. And though she instantly glanced away, it was not long before her attention returned to him.

He could feel her gaze.

A new intensity had entered it, and he wondered what she sought from him other than the promise he had given.

Following the meal, which had for once been graced by the presence of both Lord Hugh and Lady Joan at the table, the footmen moved the tables aside to make room for dancing. The harper set up at the head of the chamber and commenced to play a number of lively tunes.

The children joined in the dancing, young Emmaline with a glowing face. Tomas imagined it was only during such celebrations the children were allowed the honor of joining with the rest of the family in after-supper activities. Lord Hugh and Lady Joan sat watching, and at first both Gilliane and Eduard refused to participate, but with Lord Gervase and his sister, Lady Agnes and Lord Roger, himself and Mistress Genevieve, they made a set.

Tomas captained young Emmaline valiantly, and smiled at his other partners, but as the dance progressed, he could barely wait for the moment he faced Genevieve. When they met at last, their first few steps were stiff and courtly. Then the magic of the music wrapped around him, and when he took her hand the warmth of her touch spread through his fingers to find his heart. Her slippers whispered on the stone, and her eyes clung to his.

For an instant he forgot—forgot the dust of the Holy Land, the sickness and pain. He forgot his grief.

A smile came to Genevieve's eyes and reflected into his. Master Dennis played on and on, and when the dance parted them, he held his breath until his fingers once more met Genevieve's.

The others clapped with delight when the dance finished. The children clamored for another turn. Not until Tomas sat down did he wonder, *What would Maddox think?* Would he envy Tomas the chance to dance with his young lady? His betrothed.

Tomas had to believe not. If that truly had been Maddox speaking to him in the chapel and not some guilt-induced delusion, Tomas must believe that Maddox's generous heart had outlasted him.

No matter. He could still feel Genevieve's fingers on his, even though she no longer looked at him. It would be enough to keep him warm all the night long.

Chapter Sixteen

Genevieve sat in front of her dressing table in her bedchamber, listening to the wind chasing around the stones of the castle. Morning had come, but she could scarcely tell from the scant amount of light trickling in through the narrow window. The fire in her chamber burned fitfully, and her eyes felt heavy from lack of sleep.

It had been a fitful night withal. The rising wind and her thoughts had combined to keep her awake.

How many times had she relived that dance with Sir Tomas? The feel of his fingers on hers, the look in his dark eyes. The song Master Dennis had played while they danced and the way her body and Sir Tomas's had moved together, faultlessly in time.

She closed her eyes, savoring the memory. She'd dreamed of that dance in the few moments of sleep she'd managed to snatch.

Oh, what was she to do with these feelings? Unwanted. Inappropriate. Undeniable.

She drew toward her the tiny carved box that stood on her dressing table, and opened the lid. Inside she had tucked the small square of silk. And within that—

She took it out carefully, unfolded the scrap of fabric and placed the object thence revealed on her palm.

Worn, tattered, broken in a few places. It did not look like much, yet it was. *It was*. The symbol of the truth in a young man's heart. One he had carried far, even unto his death.

She could see his face so clearly still. The earnest blue eyes that had ever gazed with honesty into her own, filled with laughter, with admiration. With love.

He had worn this against his heart, a heart now stilled.

Tears filled her eyes and spilled over. Gilliane was right, she had not wept for him, not properly. She'd been concerned with so many other things. The weather, and providing for her guests. Mother's welfare and the grief of Maddox's parents.

Her feelings for Tomas Monmercy.

But she could not have feelings for him. She could not allow herself to. All her love and loyalty, all her devotion should belong to the young man to whom she'd been betrothed. He who'd carried this fragile heart.

Anything else would be shameful.

So she could not think of the way Sir Tomas looked at her. Of the flutter she felt in response. Of the strength of his shoulders, the breadth of his chest. The beauty of his hands or the fervent admiration in his eyes.

A scratch sounded at her chamber door. Supposing it one of the maids, she called out. "Enter." And quickly tucked the tattered heart back into the square of silk just as her cousin, Agnes, stepped in.

"Oh, my dear." Agnes hurried to Genevieve's side. She sat close on the bench, the place Mother used to sit while combing out Genevieve's hair, her blue eyes wide with concern. "You have been weeping, here all on your own. I was afraid it must be so, when I saw your face last night."

Genevieve looked askance.

"When we were all dancing," Agnes explained hastily.

"Oh." Heat stained Genevieve's skin. She had hoped she'd concealed her feelings well enough that no one else had noticed. What had Agnes seen during the set danced with Sir Tomas?

Agnes took Genevieve's hands in her own. "You have had much to deal with, Cousin. I am not surprised that you are feeling overset."

She plucked a handkerchief from her bodice and pressed it into Genevieve's hand. "Have a good cry if you will. It might help."

Genevieve wailed, "I cannot seem to stop."

Agnes let her cry for several moments before smoothing the veil back from her face. "Is it that he reminds you of Maddox? Of his absence? Or is there something more?"

Genevieve shook her head. "I have no right and no cause to feel anything more."

"Oh, my love, feelings rarely answer to what should be."

"Agnes, I cannot help believing this is all my fault. Had I not sent Maddox away on that pilgrimage—why? Why did I do so?"

"For your dear father's sake."

"But Father perished anyway. Both of them are gone."

"I know, lamb. 'Tis hard to bear."

"Gilliane, who had a sort of *tendresse* for Maddox, blames me for sending him. She hates me for it."

"I am certain that is not true."

"It comes to me now, I did not appreciate what I had." Maddox might not have been the love of her life, but how many women ever got to experience such a love? And she had loved him, dearly.

"I was so fortunate," she whispered. "I might have been sent away into marriage with a stranger. As are so many women." She turned her gaze on her cousin. "As were you."

Agnes settled back a bit on the bench. "Aye. It is true, I did not know Roger when Father arranged the marriage between us. And—and going away to marry a near-stranger was frightening. But Father chose wisely. It did not take long for affection to grow between us. By the time I birthed Justin, I was happy in the union."

"Many women are not so fortunate."

"Nay, so they are not."

"They are sent off to men twice their age, harsh strangers. Far from home." She crumpled the handkerchief in her fingers. "It was not so, for me. My— my best friend. Right here at home. The joining of two fine estates."

"Aye."

"Why could I not be content with that, Agnes?"

Her cousin's look of concern deepened. "Were you not content with the betrothal?"

"Nay. Instead of being content, I asked more of Maddox. More. In an attempt to buy time."

"Oh, Genevieve."

"I sent him from me on a quest that was near impossible to fulfill. How could I have been so selfish?"

"Oh, lass." Agnes took Genevieve into her arms. "You are aught but selfish. I have watched you worry about everyone these past days, save yourself. About Maddox's family and your dear mama. About Sir Tomas—"

Genevieve stiffened in her arms.

"Is it that, troubling you?" Agnes asked softly. "Is it him?"

Genevieve remained silent.

"My dear, listen to me. We all have such feelings. Do you think I have never looked upon a man other than Roger and thought, 'Ah, he is fine and handsome? But he is not my husband.' Marriage is ordained by God, and had you wed your Maddox, you would have been loyal to him."

"I would."

"That does not mean you cannot—well, take note of Sir Tomas. He is a very appealing man, valiant, noble, and devoted. Any woman would be a bit swept off her feet."

Genevieve escaped from her cousin's arms and sat back on the bench, mopping at her eyes. "I have no right to such feelings. All my devotion should belong to Maddox."

"Sweeting, Maddox is dead. He rests in the blessed soil of the Holy Land and will nevermore come to your door."

"Do you not see? That makes it even worse."

"Maddox was your friend from childhood. You will always love him. But you are a young woman, one connected to a sizeable estate. You must marry yet."

"I know, but I cannot think of it."

"Trust my father. He will help your mother arrange something for you when the time is right. No need to think about it as yet."

Perhaps not, but was it time to think about forgiveness? Would Maddox have forgiven her? And did she deserve to be forgiven?

Chapter Seventeen

Tomas stood inside the stable door and watched the morning sun struggle to rise. Behind him, the horses seemed content. He'd cared for them all in addition to Algernon, cleaned out their boxes and spread clean straw. Given each of them a feed. He'd loosened his muscles and warmed himself as he worked.

Still, he could see his breath puffing into the chilly air. During the night it had stopped snowing and the wind had died. Everything had frozen over.

He needed to leave soon. To stay any longer, to watch the emotions come and go on Mistress Genevieve's face, the flicker of her thoughts in her eyes, well, it had become unbearable.

He did not belong here, much as he might wish to stay. This was Maddox's place, Maddox's life, to which *Maddox* should have returned. He, Tomas, had no claim on it—on her—other than a duty already fulfilled.

Every time he thought of it, though, of leaving and never again seeing Genevieve, his heart arose in a wild protest and his mind promptly supplied half a score reasons he should stay. The roads were still too treacherous, the weather too unpredictable. He had promised Genevieve he would stay until Three Kings Day.

Roderick, the ostler, came hurrying up, his feet slipping and sliding on the ice that rimed the yard. "Sir

Tomas, I am that sorry to be late. Were ye waiting for your mount?" The man's forehead creased. "Ye are never leaving us so soon?"

"Nay, not just yet. And you needn't hurry. I've cared for the beasts inside."

Roderick looked perplexed. "Sir, I've told ye that will never do. Ye be a guest of ours."

"And I've told you I need to be busy, and I enjoy the work." Tomas gave the man a closer look. "Is all well with you, Roderick?"

"To say true, sir, we did not get much sleep upstairs. 'Tis the lad. He seems to be feeling poorly."

"Ralph?" Tomas had developed an affection for the boy, who was bright and winsome.

"Aye. 'Tis the time o' year for the young ones to take ill, and the weather has been that vile. Half the time his feet are wet." He made a face. "Just like mine."

Tomas nodded. "A bit of the grippe?"

"I am certain 'tis all it is."

"Does he need aught? I am sure Mistress Genevieve would—"

"By the saints, m'lord, pray do not trouble her with it. She has enough on her hands."

"To be sure. How do you think the roads look?"

Roderick shook his head. "Not good. All that snow we got has melted and refrozen, then frozen again. There's water under that ice, now."

"No fit condition for travel?"

"I fear not, sir." Roderick's troubled eyes found Tomas's face. "I know Master Maddox's parents are eager to go home. They may need to stay put a while yet."

"*Oui.* You knew Master Maddox, did you,

Roderick?"

"Oh, aye, sir." Roderick's face softened. "From a young sprog. As fine a young man as ever grew. We were happy at the thought of him as master here." Roderick's gaze filled with grief. "The others are saying you were with him, sir, when he died."

"So I was."

"I hope he had a peaceful end."

It could not be called that. And yet once Maddox had pressed the mistletoe heart into Tomas's hand and received his promise, he had achieved a measure of relief.

"The Holy Land is full of pestilence, and every kind of fever you can imagine."

"Yet our brave King Richard Lionheart is there even now, fighting, is he not, sir?"

"So he is."

"And you, m'lord. By fighting there, as they say, you have earned your way into Heaven."

Had he? But he might well forsake his claim to Heaven for the smile in Mistress Genevieve's eyes.

****

He had hope of glimpsing that smile far sooner than he expected. He was knocking the snow mixed with mud from the stables off his boots, just inside the back door, when he looked up and beheld her, only an arm's length away from him.

"Oh." Her eyes widened. "It is you, Sir Tomas. Have you been out to look at the road?"

"*Oui*. Impassible as yet, I am afraid."

She bit her lip. "Lady Joan will be sore disappointed. Here…" She indicated a bench just behind him. "Sit. I will help you off with those boots."

"Mistress, I cannot permit—you will soil your hands."

"And then I may wash them. Sit."

He did so, half bemused by her forcefulness, and she knelt at his feet. He watched her, barely breathing, as she bent to the task, setting his boots carefully aside.

"I will ask Wilfred to clean those for you."

"Thank you, Mistress."

"Now come to breakfast."

He padded after her in his stocking feet as she led the way past the kitchen door, stopping in the scullery to clean her hands.

"It is only the two of us so early," she remarked as they entered the hall. "But there is pottage and something warm to drink."

He sat, and she took the place opposite him. With no servants in attendance, she served him with her own hands.

"I was thinking," he remarked then. "It is not far from here to the DeVille estate, is that correct?"

"Only a few miles. I have walked it, the shorter distance through the orchards, more times than I can count."

"I could perhaps escort the DeVilles thence, as soon as travel is possible. I know how anxious Lady Joan is to go home. Thus should they bog down on the way, I will be there to assist their driver and young Master Eduard, to make sure they get free."

She gave him a steady look. "That is very kind of you."

"There is not enough I can do for them."

"I am sure they would appreciate it."

"Then once they reach home safely, I may ride

south."

"Ride south?"

He gazed at her pointedly. "To the port at Sutton, and eventually home."

Her fingers tensed on the edge of the table. "Leave, you mean."

"It is time, Mistress Genevieve."

"But—" Was that protest he saw in her eyes? "You agreed to stay until Three Kings Day."

"So I did. And I regret—regret that I cannot. You must see, Mistress Genevieve, things have changed since I gave you that agreement."

"Have they?"

"My—my feelings have changed. I fear they have become…" He sought for the word. "Inappropriate. I would do nothing to upset Maddox's family, nor to come between you and his memory."

Color flooded Genevieve's face, but her eyes did not dodge his.

"I understand. I will be desolated, Sir Tomas, if you—"

"Well, this is cozy." Gilliane swung into the room. "Two early risers together, is it?"

Sir Tomas stood and presented a bow, striving to disguise his disappointment at the interruption. Genevieve's young sister gave him a hard-eyed stare. He needed to be far less perceptive than he was to miss the fact that she harbored resentment toward him.

Just like young Master Eduard.

She shot him a hard look. "The rest of my family members are still abed. It seems only those wishing to meet in secret would rise so early."

"Mind your manners, Gilliane," Genevieve scolded.

"And keep a civil tongue toward our guest."

Tomas, who had reseated himself, gave her a nod. "I assure you, Mistress Gilliane, nothing untoward has happened here."

Her glare did not ease. "Not here, perhaps. I hope, Sir Tomas, you are making plans to depart. You must feel how awkward your presence is making things for Eduard and his family."

"Gilliane!" Genevieve flushed. "How dare you say such a thing?"

"Well, 'tis true! He is a constant reminder of what Maddox suffered, and how he failed to come home—though Sir Tomas managed to make it and to save his own skin."

Tomas said, "I understand that Eduard believes I failed his brother somehow, in the Holy Land. He has made that clear."

"Aye, and I agree with him!" Pain, pure and simple, shone in Gilliane's brown eyes. "He was the dearest man on earth and should have been protected by one claiming to be a chevalier."

"I agree with you. I should have protected him, as all pilgrims to the Holy City."

Gillian's lips trembled. "Then why, when I came in, did I hear Genevieve say she would be devastated to lose your company?"

Tomas glanced at Genevieve, who appeared mortified. "Your sister merely expressed once more the hospitality I have been offered since I arrived."

"I suppose so." Gilliane swept Tomas with a look up and down. "'Tis common decency, which my father taught us to afford. You just be certain, Sir Knight, you remember it is that and nothing more."

Chapter Eighteen

"Sir Tomas, Lord Gervase tells me you have offered to escort me and my family home safely. If that is so, I would be more than happy to accept the offer."

Lord Hugh paused, upon entering the hall that evening, to address Tomas who had just come in from outside.

Tomas gave him a small bow. "I would be more than happy to be of service to you and your family, Lord Hugh."

Lord Hugh gazed at Tomas steadily. "My wife is anxious to return home. When we arrived here to celebrate Christmas with our good friends, I believe she half expected Maddox to arrive some time before the feast of the Three Kings. He did so promise, last year, and my son was a man who kept his promises."

"This I did learn of him. Her hopes must indeed have been high." Tomas hesitated, sorrow filling him. "I regret that I am the one who arrived instead."

"Do not say that. We are both grateful you were such a good companion to Maddox. But my good wife wishes to retire with her grief."

"Of course."

"When we traveled here, I fear I was incautious. Since the distance was so short, I brought no servants except our driver and my lady's maid. We have never had need of an escort on that friendly stretch of road.

"Now, however, I fear getting bogged down with no one save our driver, myself, and young Eduard to push us out again. 'Twould almost be easier to walk, but I fear my lady could not manage it."

"She should not try. I have just been looking at the road once more, *monsieur*." He would not add that his own conflicted feelings drove him to a desire for escape. It grew more and more difficult to see Genevieve while knowing that he should not, could not touch her.

"Do you deem the roads passable?"

In truth, Tomas did not, the one out from the estate no more than two ruts filled with half-frozen water and slush. He would not yet consider traveling south for the port of Sutton. But that was not what Sir Hugh proposed.

"You say 'tis not far to travel, over the roads?"

"Not far at all."

"Then depending on the weather overnight, I believe we may make the attempt come morning."

"Thank you." Lord Hugh clasped Tomas's arm. "And, I thought you might like to see Maddox's home, of which he no doubt told you much."

"He did, Lord Hugh."

"You are welcome to stay with us, Sir Tomas, for as long as you like."

A way out. It was a way out of this tangle in which he found himself. He could gather his few possessions and relocate with Maddox's family to their estate and wait for better weather before traveling south, and home. But he could not imagine Eduard would welcome his company, not with the way that young man even now darted poisonous looks at him from the other side of the chamber.

Not valued at home, not welcomed at Maddox's

estate, and certainly not able to stay here much longer—there was no place in all the wide world for him. He'd survived the Holy Land, *oui*, but for what?

"I would not like to intrude upon you, Sir Hugh, in your time of sorrow."

"My wife would be most glad of the company. The three of us will just rattle around in that great house now."

Tomas nodded soberly, not willing to toss Sir Hugh's hospitality back in his face. "I will be more than glad to escort you to your estate, Lord Hugh. And I will decide then whether I can remain longer away from home."

****

Something, so Genevieve remained convinced, was yet amiss at Clarendon. She just could not seem to put her finger on what it was. She could sense discord in the very air, as if it rolled along the chilly stone passageways and hovered in the corners of the rooms like unnoticed, additional guests. This new instinct she had birthed, that which was somehow connected to Sir Tomas, screamed aloud about it.

Though, to be sure, the disharmony did not originate with him. The adults in the party all seemed edgy, which might be due to the weather or to inactivity, now that many of the Christmas festivities had passed. The visitors felt trapped by the weather. Eduard's face looked like that of a bad-tempered bull, and Gilliane kept shooting Genevieve resentful and accusing glances.

Perhaps the discord, or a large part of it, originated with Genevieve herself. Perhaps the guilt she felt—that fed by her sister and kept burning steadily by her own self-accusations—made her imagine that everyone else felt as unhappy as she.

Yet Sir Tomas…

Sir Tomas still seemed to be holding himself aloof from her. She'd seen him come in from the near dark and watched Lord Hugh stop him at the door of the hall for a word. The exchange had been brief and sober. Both men had nodded.

Thereafter, Tomas refused to meet Genevieve's gaze. It frustrated her, and caused the breath to clench in her throat. She hadn't liked it the last time he'd treated her this way, and had hoped they'd moved beyond it. She enjoyed catching his eye, watching the fervent light flash there. She waited with bated breath for his smile.

Which made a very good reason why she should follow his lead, and avoid him as much as possible. Had she not just finished assuring herself she, of all women, did not deserve nor warrant such attentions?

If she forgot, Gilliane would surely remind her. Again.

Gilliane was right. Here she sat, bereaved of her betrothed and in mourning, and all she could think to do was miss the attentions of a handsome young man. She should be ashamed.

But, Heaven help her, as they began the evening meal she could not keep her eyes from following the movements of his hands, from clinging to his lips when he spoke, or from marking the light that filled his eyes when he smiled.

Lord Hugh sat at table with them though Lady Joan had once more remained in her chamber. During the first course, he said, "I wish to let you know, Lady Maude, and Mistress Genevieve, my family and I will be leaving you come morning. Sir Tomas has kindly agreed to see us safe home."

Mother immediately began to exclaim, saying she would be sad to see them go, but Genevieve sat silent while waves of shock and protest washed over her.

Leaving. He was leaving. Surely, surely after seeing Maddox's family home, he meant to retrace his steps to Clarendon.

She turned her gaze on him. Still, he did not return her glance.

"Sir Tomas," she blurted, "I hope you plan to come back afterward, to return to us here."

He did look at her then. She beheld the regret in his eyes and knew the answer even before he spoke.

"I have enjoyed my stay here, Mistress Genevieve, and I am more grateful for your welcome than I may express. But I do believe it is time for me to be on my way."

"But—"

Her protest was lost amid those of the children, with whom Sir Tomas was a favorite, and of Mother, who quite sincerely bade him know he was more than welcome to stay.

Gilliane's gaze pinioned Genevieve, as if daring her to make a further request. Uncle Gervase also shot her a look. Did he hear the words she could not utter?

You agreed to stay until Three Kings Day. You do not break your promises.

Perhaps Sir Tomas heard, for he spoke as if to her alone. "I know you very kindly invited me to stay throughout the holy season. But—well, things have changed."

Had they? Oh, aye. If she were half so honest as she wanted to be, she could not deny it. Her attraction to this earnest and valiant man was very nearly out of hand.

He was right. He must leave her. But oh, oh, how would she bear it, over and above all the other things she had to bear?

She should not still have a heart to be broken. Were she truly the woman others thought her, it would already be shattered by the loss of Maddox, who'd loved her so truly unto his last breath.

The meal continued, and Genevieve strove mightily to play the role of hostess. But now it was she who fled Tomas's gaze and dodged that of Gilliane.

Too many eyes here. Too many chances for them to see what this news had done to her.

Still, she must speak to Tomas. Somehow, she must find the opportunity for a word alone with him. He might see Maddox's parents home, aye. It was the sort of generous and caring thing he would do. But naught said he had to remain away forevermore.

He must come back to her. Even though she had no right to ask. Even if it went beyond the bounds of decency.

She had to make him see, against all likelihood and propriety, that he must return.

Chapter Nineteen

Genevieve spent much of that night in prayer and secretly hoping for the weather to worsen, even though she suspected that was quite likely a sin. She lay in her bed listening for the wind, but it had died to a mere murmur. She beseeched the heavens for the sound of sleet striking against the stones of the castle.

She examined her own soul.

Only at moments such as this did she allow herself to look deep within—in the night when all was quiet and nobody else knew. She'd done so for years, and far more often since sending Maddox away.

But she'd believed he'd come back. Deep down, she had. He'd been part of her life for as long as she could remember, the neighbor lad with the sunny smile who always, always returned.

Except this time.

She thought of him dying so far away from her, from his family who adored him, alone save for the companion met in a prison cell. He'd been there for her sake. His death rested on her conscience.

Would she have sent him if she'd known she would never see him again? No. *No.* She would instead have kept him close. Cherished him.

As a friend.

She turned over, restless in her bed. She had loved her father dearly, enough to pray fervently that he might recover from his dire illness. She'd loved Maddox too. But not the way he'd wanted her to.

Lying there in the dark room, she acknowledged she'd never been in love. She hadn't even understood what that meant.

Until now.

Was she in love with Tomas Monmercy?

The longing in her heart whispered *aye*. Her head argued she could not possibly be in love with a man she scarcely knew. Not as she'd known Maddox, able to sense his moods and anticipate every smile. She had no right to fall in love.

She did not deserve love, not after what she'd done.

Falling in love was a frivolous idea. A woman could not expect it, in marriage. A woman married for rank or to increase an estate, as she would have done. Love came later, if she was very fortunate. It grew over the years.

That had happened for her parents. And for Maddox's parents, from all she could see. For Agnes and Roger also.

How dare she think she deserved more? She did not. She did not deserve it, but having met Sir Tomas, she wanted it for her own.

Oh, how was she to face the morning? How say a farewell to him?

She captured no more than an hour's sleep before morning, and awoke with a heavy head.

She arose and went directly to her window. A rime of frost on the diamond panes made it impossible to see out. but she could feel the cold seeping in.

Maybe they would change their minds about traveling today.

She dressed and hurried downstairs, only to find

almost no one other than the servants astir.

Only one of her guests was awake. She met him near the front door where he entered on a sweep of icy air that stirred the shadows here, where there wasn't much light. Genevieve knew him without seeing him clearly.

"Sir Tomas?"

"Mademoiselle Genevieve." He paused where he stood just inside the entry, his heavy cloak making him look overly large in the gloom. Genevieve could smell the cold on him, and it seemed she could feel his emotions tumbling through him, as if they were her own. As if this man, this one man, unlikely as it might seem, were the other half of her. The reply to all her thoughts. Her perfect match.

Suddenly breathless, she asked, "Have you been out looking at the roads?"

"*Oui.*"

"Will you—will you be able to travel?"

"I believe so. Everything has frozen over during the night. It will be treacherous, but if it is what Sir Hugh and Lady Joan wish, I will get them through." For Maddox's sake. He did not add that. He did not have to.

She reached out, unable to prevent herself from doing so. Alone there in the entry, who could see?

"I do not wish for you to go." Oh, by all that was holy, had those words come from her?

His eyes widened. "Mistress Genevieve—"

"I know, I should not say so. But I cannot keep silent." She drew a desperate breath into her lungs. "Please—please say you will return, once you have seen them home."

She had no right to seek such a promise from him, after disastrously asking one of Maddox. But then, if he did not promise, she might never see this man again.

He clasped her outstretched hand in both of his. His fingers felt cold and strong.

He raised her fingers to his lips. "Mademoiselle Genevieve, you know I am devoted to you, and to your wishes."

She went dizzy. He would agree. He would return to her. That meant she could go on breathing.

"But," he said, "I do not believe it would be a wise decision for me to return to Clarendon."

It felt as if someone had struck her. The only thing keeping her upright was the strength of Tomas's grip.

"Why?" But she knew. She knew as well as he did.

Gravely he told her, "I have feelings for you, Mademoiselle Genevieve. Feelings that in the circumstances are utterly inappropriate."

"Aye." Determinedly, she captured his gaze there in the gloom even as the heat flooded her skin. "I have those same feelings, so I fear, toward you."

He whispered, "You belong to Maddox. His dearest treasure. How could I violate his great trust in me?"

Maddox is dead. She didn't say that. But it throbbed unspoken in the air between them.

"Is it not enough," he asked, "that I am here and he is not, though it was his most devout wish?"

Guilt. Tomas felt it, even as she did.

Must she give up this love she felt for the sake of it? Watch him walk out through that door for good?

"Nay," she whispered and leaned toward him. He still had one of her hands clasped in both of his, held against his chest. She placed her other hand on his cheek and went up on her tiptoes.

His eyes widened.

Tearing her gaze from his, she looked up into the shadows that cloaked the top of the doorway. And up. There, where one of the footmen had hung it, a bit of greenery dangled from the stonework.

She'd urged them to put up the greenery this year, including the mistletoe, wanting the holy days to be as they'd always been. She'd given the household servants free rein with it and had no way of knowing a sprig of mistletoe hung here.

Yet it did. *It did.*

Last year, Maddox had claimed a kiss under the mistletoe, just inside the great hall. What woman would deny the taking of such? She'd fashioned for him the mistletoe heart.

This time despite the fear, the guilt and the uncertainty, it was her turn.

"Sir Tomas, will you deny me one, only one kiss?"

Chapter Twenty

Tomas knew very well he should step away. Make some courteous excuse. Release Mistress Genevieve's fingers from his hold and leave this dim entryway where the cold air swirled around them.

Where they remained isolated, alone.

It was what a decent man would do, and he liked to think of himself as a decent man still, despite—despite the way he felt about this woman.

Another man's beloved. Not just another man, but one he'd come to admire and respect. A friend, down to his very soul.

Yet—yet he too loved Genevieve and it was one kiss, claimed beneath the mistletoe.

His feet rooted to the stones of the floor, he gazed into Genevieve's eyes. Pale gray and luminous in the dim light, they beseeched him for something he could quite easily give.

One kiss. Could he deny it to her? To himself?

She stood on her tiptoes, her fingers pressed against his cold cheek, her lips but a breath from his.

"Forgive me," he whispered—to the air, and perhaps to Maddox—before he claimed those lips with his own.

He meant it for a mere mark of respect, of affection. A granting of her request and nothing more. As soon as their mouths met, though, light exploded in his head. A glorious light it was, warm and holy.

How could something this pure and sweet be wrong?

Genevieve sighed, a breath she breathed into him, and leaned closer. All at once her warmth became his own, her body beneath the brocade robes she wore, the intensity of her emotions. Desire came an instant later and flooded all his senses.

Not just a mark of affection, then. Not just a kiss.

The hand she had laid against his cheek crept up around his neck and plunged into his hair. His heart beat so hard, she must be able to feel it through their clasped fingers.

She parted her lips beneath his and he dared to enter her. To taste. To claim. He must memorize this—the taste and the feel of her. He must remember because it could never, never happen again.

She clung to him when he lifted his mouth from hers. She trembled. His head buzzed so he could barely hear himself when he said again, "Forgive me."

"There is naught to forgive."

Didn't she realize he spoke not to her?

Her body still pressed close to his, she whispered, "Do not go. Please do not leave me."

"Mistress, I must. Maddox's parents—they need me."

She drew back just far enough to gaze once more into his eyes. "I know. I know they do."

"I have a duty to do for them as Maddox would wish. As he cannot."

Her gaze did not waver from his. It did not duck or hide. "What if I also need you?"

That—that was another thing altogether. Would Maddox assign him the duty of loving his bride in his stead?

"Genevieve—"

"At least say you will come back to me."

A deep sadness filled him. Was that not what she'd told Maddox? Oh, maybe not in those exact words or with the same sentiment. But how many times had Maddox relived for him, while they languished in their barren cell, the moment she had gifted him the mistletoe heart?

And he'd promised to return.

"Genevieve," he breathed her name. Never, never had he felt like this. Weak before his desire for her, and at the same time incredibly strong. He must be strong enough to do what he believed was right. But what about the love he felt for her?

"I will try," he said at last. "But—but I will not promise. Because I have seen the troubles of this world, and what such a promise can cost the giver."

Her fingers, still in his hair, tightened. "Fair enough. I can ask no more." Quite suddenly her eyes filled with tears. He watched them flood and gather on her lashes when she attempted to blink them away.

"It will wound me, Tomas Monmercy, watching you ride away. But I believe—believe you will do your best to return."

"My lady."

Her hand still in his, he stepped away from her and dropped to one knee. He bowed his head to her, and pressed her hand to his heart.

He could feel her, thus. Feel her gaze upon his hair, feel the tension in her hands. Feel all her troubled emotions.

Did she love him? He could not say. Did he love

her? *Oui*, oh, *oui*.

He got to his feet and thought he saw a shadow move in the corner of his eye. He whirled about toward the archway into the hall, and Genevieve followed. Someone stood there—but it was only Rex, who came forward to Genevieve, his great tail sweeping in an arc.

"Oh, Rex," she breathed, and the hound came and pressed close to her. She bent her face and hid it in the gray fur.

Tomas stepped past them, his boots sounding on the stone, and left them standing beneath the sprig of mistletoe.

****

Genevieve dared not tell anyone. She could never say what had passed between her and Tomas in the cold and drafty entryway. What had been asked, and given. She could not let herself react when Tomas and Maddox's family prepared to leave later that morning.

Nor could she share with anyone that after Tomas had walked away from her, she'd dragged a bench over beneath the sprig of mistletoe and, with Rex watching anxiously, climbed up and stretched perilously high to break off a sprig.

She would tell no one she had it even now, tucked inside her chemise close against her heart.

Mistletoe, as she knew, had a dubious history. In ancient times, here in Britain, it was considered a sacred plant, since it grew not on the earth but halfway to the spiritual realm. It had been much sought and harvested with reverence by the druids.

In Norse times—and she being of Norman descent, as had been Maddox himself, carried a measure of Norse blood—it had been considered a sign of bad luck, because it had brought about the death of the beloved Norse god, Baldur.

How had it changed from that to the right to claim a kiss? She did not know, but she was glad, glad it did.

To Maddox, the kiss had represented constancy. She could only hope, if it retained any lingering, ancient magic, it would bring Tomas back to her again.

She must put the emotions away from her, and all her hope with them for the time. She must go downstairs, oversee the household, and act like her heart had not been torn from her breast.

She must see to her guests and bid Maddox's family goodbye.

She had a score of duties that must come before her own despair. Her own pain.

Do not despair, she told herself. Even while you watch him ride away from you, you must keep faith that, against all odds, he will return.

Chapter Twenty-One

Genevieve did not know where to look when the farewells were said. Mother embraced both Sir Hugh and Lady Joan, and a few tears were shed. Genevieve embraced Lady Joan also, and looking around to bid Eduard goodbye, saw him standing in conversation with Gilliane, their heads nearly touching. A strange sight among so many other troubling ones—in the past the two of them had barely been able to tolerate one another. Perhaps, she thought, Maddox's loss had moved them beyond such petty differences as they had once espoused.

Throughout all the leave-taking, Sir Tomas stood silent. At the entrance to the hall, Uncle Gervase turned to him.

"Young man, it has been an honor to meet and to know you." To Genevieve's surprise, her uncle embraced Tomas, thumping him on the back. "A safe journey to you. You go with our gratitude."

Mother stepped forward and clasped Tomas's hands. "Thank you for being such a good friend to Maddox. You are most welcome to return here any time."

"My lady." He bowed deeply over her hand, so deeply the black curls tumbled over his brow. "You are kindness itself."

"We must be off," Sir Hugh announced, "while yet

the weather holds. Thank you all for your hospitality."

The footmen struggled out with the luggage. The DeVilles' wagon had already been brought around and stood in a thin beam of sunshine, the two stout ponies hitched. Both the driver and Lady Joan's maid waited.

Tomas's horse, Algernon, also stood ready. There were no more minutes left to Genevieve.

She did look at him then—at last—and found his dark eyes steady on her face. Her pulse leaped, and she felt again his fingers clutching her own, and the press of his lips on hers, the warmth and the magic.

But this was no magical story. It was her life, and no place for wild imaginings.

So she dropped her eyes and saw only his boots as he turned away and went out slowly, with Lady Joan on his arm.

Though she had no cloak or shawl, Genevieve followed.

Snow and a rime of ice dusted the top steps. They were steep and treacherous, and Tomas half carried Lady Joan down.

The wind caught Genevieve's skirts and blew them out behind her as she watched Tomas and Eduard safely stow Lady Joan and her maid in the enclosed wagon.

The driver, a stout man well bundled against the cold, was already on the bench. Tomas swung up on his mount and called to the driver, "Let me ride on ahead. I can assess the condition of the road for the wagon."

The man waved.

Genevieve went breathless. He was about to ride away. She was losing him.

Rex ran out the open door behind her. Mother called to her to come away in out of the cold.

Genevieve remained where she was. At the last moment, before Tomas urged the huge warhorse forward, he turned his head and looked at her. One last, burning look that pierced her clear through. Worth waiting for, even in the stinging cold.

"Genevieve," Uncle Gervase it was who called now, "come in."

Fingers caught at Genevieve from behind. Uncle Gervase, no doubt wishing to relieve Mother's fretting, urged her in.

"The roads look bad," Genevieve said as she let her uncle lead her to the hall. "Do you think they will make a safe journey?"

Mother replied, "I pray so. And if the way becomes too hazardous, I trust they will have the good sense to turn around and come right back to Clarendon."

Was there hope of that? Genevieve caught her breath.

Mother put an arm around Genevieve's shoulders and urged her closer to the fire that roared in the hearth.

"My daughter, I know how fond you are of Maddox's family, how dear they are to you. But try not to worry. I am certain if anyone can get them home safely, it is young Sir Tomas."

"Aye," Agnes agreed, tossing Genevieve a meaningful look. "What a sterling young man he is."

"My dear, you are shaking." Mother scolded, "I told you not to stand out in the cold. I hope you have not taken a chill."

"I am fine, Mother." Only she was not, and might never again be.

****

Sir Tomas and his charges did not return. Genevieve

surrendered any hope of it reluctantly, and with regret.

Regret, these days, seemed to be her constant companion.

Now everyone's mood lowered. Mother had gone quiet, and Gilliane brooded by herself at the end of the table. Thank heavens for Master Dennis, who did his best to lend a spattering of bright conversation, and for Emmaline and Justin, who likely did not understand the situation well enough to feel lowered in their spirits.

The two of them kept the others occupied with their games and laughter. But Genevieve must have made half a score trips to the door, to check the weather and see if she could catch a glimpse of any travelers.

Agnes kept an eye on her, as did Gilliane, if a far less sympathetic one. By nightfall, she estimated the DeVilles and their escort must have reached home. She had to lecture herself sternly to keep from continuing her watch out the front.

So many times she had walked that distance, both over the roads and, as she'd told Tomas, through the orchards. That being so, she reckoned that if the wagon bogged down, the party would walk the rest of the way home, even if Tomas and the driver had to carry Lady Joan.

Travel in winter was never a good bet, which meant she'd once again erred in judgment by inviting guests for the holy days. She'd placed the joy of it, to her and to Mother, before the safety of those dear to her.

Just as with Maddox.

Shortly after nightfall, Cook came to her. It seemed strange seeing Cora outside her domain of the kitchen, and Genevieve, who had been on her way up to the solar to retrieve Mother's shawl, stopped and stared.

"Mistress Cora? Is something amiss?"

"The ostler's young son, Mistress. He is very bad."

"Ralph, do you mean?" Genevieve's eyes widened. "I thought 'twas but a touch of the grippe."

"So did his mother." Cook's round face looked troubled. "But he's worse now, and raving. His young sister says she feels unwell also."

"Perhaps a poultice. Have they tried that?"

"Aye, mistress. A mixture on the lad's chest. If we could have a barber to bleed him—"

"I fear we cannot. Travel is too difficult."

Mother stepped out from the main hall. "Genevieve? What is it?"

"Roderick's young son is worse. A fever." Swiftly, Genevieve made up her mind. "I will go to him."

"My dear, you must not. A winter sickness so early in the year, it is a terrible sign. What if you too take ill?"

"I will be fine, Mother. We have some herbs," Genevieve told Cook. "I can burn those for him. I am sure he will soon recover."

But when she saw Ralph in the low-ceilinged quarters above the stable, fear stirred in her heart.

Winter was indeed a dire time for sickness. And she could not help but think such misfortune came in threes. First Father, then Maddox and—young Ralph?

The ostler's wife, Rachel, had put the boy to rest in her own bed and piled what must be every blanket the family owned atop him. All that showed was a flushed face and a crop of brown hair.

Rachel greeted Genevieve with an anxious, "Mistress," followed by a spate of words. "You see how he is. Oh, mistress, what's to be done?"

"I am certainly no barber or physician, Rachel, but I

will take a look at him."

Uncle Gervase, who had insisted on accompanying Genevieve to the stable quarters, touched her arm.

"Not too close, as your good mother said. There will be ill humors."

"I do not fear for myself."

She approached the bed, recalling the lad who just a few days ago had run and played in the snow. His skin bore not only the flush of fever but an angry rash.

"Rachel, does this rash reach everywhere upon his skin?"

"Aye, mistress, onto his back and chest."

"We will burn these herbs. Perhaps purifying the air will chase the fever out. Keep bathing his head and making sure he takes broth, if you have it."

"Cook sent some, mistress."

"I hope you do not mind," Roderick said quickly. "Cook's son and our Ralph are such friends—"

"Of course I do not mind." Despite her worry, Genevieve smiled at him. "If there is aught else you need, more food, or fuel for your fire, you need only ask."

Roderick bowed. "Mistress, you are kind."

Genevieve turned to the ostler's small daughter, no more than five or six, who watched all this with frightened eyes. "Elspet? I hear you are not feeling well either."

"Mistress," the child whispered. "My throat aches, as does my head."

Genevieve looked at Rachel. "Has she any spots?"

"Just a few on her chest."

Genevieve summoned a smile for the girl. "I want for you to rest alongside your brother and have some of

Cook's fine broth. Can you do that?"

"Aye, mistress."

"Try not to worry," Genevieve told Rachel and Roderick. "Call me at once if either of them grows worse."

She and Uncle Gervase walked out silently. In the stable yard they paused and looked at one another.

"Oh, Uncle, I do not like the look of that."

"Nor I, Genevieve. Let us get inside. The wind has sharpened abominably."

"You go ahead, Uncle. I wish to visit the chapel and say a prayer for those two dear children."

Chapter Twenty-Two

Time after time, when the wagon bogged down in the ruts of the road, Tomas feared they would never get it free. The ruts were deep and filled with not only frozen water but slush. The big, heavy wheels of the wagon sank down to their hubs.

To be sure, he spent more time off Algernon's back than upon it. In the end, Sir Hugh took the reins. Tomas, the driver—whose name was Wilt—and young Eduard pushed the heavy wagon out again and again, while Algernon, a reliable and biddable beast, followed along.

Long before they reached the DeVille estate, it began to snow, if snow it could be called—icy flakes flying before the cold wind. By the time the wagon bogged down at last upon the lane that led to the manor, Tomas was plastered with mud up past his knees, scraped raw, bruised, and exhausted.

He lifted Lady Joan and her maid from the cart and placed Lady Joan on Algernon's back, where she huddled most fearfully.

"Sir Tomas, I have never been up so high."

"Please, madame, do not worry. He is quite gentle." For a war horse.

Algernon picked his way up the trail to the manor, a large building which Tomas was in no fit state to appreciate at the time. No sooner had he breathed a sigh of relief, seeing a number of servants hurry out to meet them, than Eduard gave a cry.

Thinking the young man had hurt himself while putting his shoulder to the wagon back in the road, Tomas turned to him in concern.

Eduard had thrown the hood of his cloak back onto his shoulders and stood four-square facing Tomas, his sword in his hand and a sneer on his face.

Tomas stared. After struggling for hours alongside the boy, the last thing he expected at the end of the journey, when they were both battered and half beaten, was some sort of challenge. And he could not imagine why Eduard would draw upon him.

Only, he could.

Even before Eduard cried out, before Lord Hugh had time to protest or Lady Joan to exclaim, Tomas's heart told him what must come. Sorrow enfolded him. Not this. Not Maddox's brother.

"Face me! You will face me, you treacherous, lack-honor Frenchman! Draw your sword and face me!"

"I cannot. I will not."

"Why? Are you a coward as well as a betrayer?"

"Eduard!" Lord Hugh thundered. "How dare you draw upon a guest?"

"He is not a guest." Eduard tossed his mop of fair hair, now sodden and splashed with mud. At that moment, for some reason, he looked more like Maddox than ever before. The sorrow in Tomas's heart deepened.

Ignoring Lord Hugh, he bowed to Eduard. "If you want your satisfaction, take it. I will not raise my sword to you."

Eyes wide and desperate, Eduard hollered, "Raise your sword, damn you, or I will kill you where you stand!"

So it came to this. The spirits, the angels, or God himself had decided after all to hand out the punishment Tomas deserved. He said to the young man, "You cannot blame me for Maddox's death more than I blame myself."

"It should have been he who survived that imprisonment. It should have been he who came home!" A wail.

"I agree. Of the two of us, I wish it had been Maddox who came home. To Mistress Genevieve. To your parents, and to you."

"He was fine and good." The sword, which extended straight at Tomas, trembled in Eduard's hand. "He did not deserve to die!"

"You are right, *monsieur*. He did not."

"Eduard!" Lord Hugh stepped forward and put himself between his son and Tomas. "What is all this about? Son, I understand and share your grief, but Sir Tomas—"

"It is his fault Maddox never came home. If he were half the knight he claims to be, he would have defended and protected our Maddox. Instead, he tries even now to take what Maddox valued above all else. Gilliane saw him and Genevieve in the hallway at Clarendon. Kissing! I will have justice on Maddox's behalf."

Everyone now stared at Tomas, including the avid servants. Lady Joan spoke numbly. "Is this true? Sir Tomas?"

"My lady, it is."

The silence became so profound, Tomas could hear the icy flakes of snow striking the ground. Tears now streamed down Eduard's face.

"Betrayer!" he accused again. "Maddox would have

done anything for love of Genevieve. As he did! He gave his very life. And you would steal her away."

Tomas held up his hands. "I would not. Mistress Genevieve and I but bid one another a fond farewell—"

"I cry foul!" Eduard howled. "And I stand here in my brother's place. If you have any honor, you will face me in his stead."

Face him. A boy of no more than fifteen years, and Tomas a hardened knight who had seen service of the worst kind in the Holy Land, who had faced torment, starvation, and imprisonment.

Slowly, slowly, Tomas drew his sword. He would let Eduard best him. Oh, he would make a show of it, to allow the lad his honor, but it would end with Eduard's sword at his throat. Here, in the slush in front of Maddox's boyhood home.

Justice, my friend? He spoke to Maddox in his mind. *I am sorry. I love her even as you did. And that I could not prevent.*

With a howl, Eduard directed a crashing blow at him, one that almost overset the boy and sent him tripping over his own feet. If he had half as much mud on his boots as did Tomas, his feet must feel heavy as stones. With the blow, Eduard left himself so wide open, Tomas could have got inside his arm and gutted him. Instead, he parried the blow with his sword and took the impact almost without thought.

Both Lord Hugh and Lady Joan cried out. Lady Joan half fell from Algernon's back and ran to her husband. "Stop them! My lord, you must stop them!"

Lord Hugh, who had hastily vacated his place between Eduard and Tomas, now drew his wife even farther out of the way.

"You did not value him!" Eduard screeched, desperate with grief. "You did not defend him! You did not protect him!"

Each accusation came accompanied by a blow. Tomas accepted both forms of attack, feeling Eduard's anger, hurt, and pain. He did not return the blows, but stepped back and back again, leading Eduard's attack away from those standing by, and away from Algernon.

The lad must tire soon. He put more strength into the blows than he should rightfully have left, after their arduous journey. Carefully Tomas stepped off the ledge that led to the house stairs and onto the edge of the driveway itself, parrying blow after blow.

And slipped on a ridge of slush that slid away beneath his feet and cast him flat on his back in the wet and cold.

The last thing he saw was Eduard's furious face, red with anger and streaked with tears, and the sword rising to begin the arc that would take Tomas's life.

Chapter Twenty-Three

Tomas must have hit his head hard on the ground when he went down, because after that glimpse of Eduard's countenance he saw stars, and then only darkness. His other senses, though, were working properly. He could hear people shouting—Lord Hugh's voice, and Eduard's, still. Lady Joan weeping. Then that too faded, into silence.

He could smell the cell, the one he and Maddox had shared together. A stench like no other, consisting of human waste, dry sand and fetid stone. He could smell the man who sat beside him—after so many weeks, they both reeked. His companion. His friend.

I would that you could see her, Tomas. A glimpse of her bonny face. One single look from her beautiful eyes. I do not doubt you would be as enchanted as I am myself.

I have seen her, Maddox, and you are right. I am stricken. Stricken with love. He could not open his eyes, could not see his companion.

Ah, and who could blame you?

Your brother blames me. He thinks I should have won your way home.

No man could do that. Only God decides which of us lives or dies.

"Eduard, hold!"

The cry came real and immediate. Tomas's eyes flew open to find he lay still on his back, his arms

136

outflung in the slush of the driveway. Eduard, his face twisted by hate and grief, unrecognizable, loomed above him, the point of his sword at Tomas's throat.

"Eduard!" Lord Hugh roared again. "Son!"

Eduard tore his gaze from Tomas's face and looked at his father, who held out his arms. After a moment that lasted forever, Eduard withdrew his sword from Tomas's throat and stumbled over Tomas's legs into Lord Hugh's arms.

The driver stepped to Tomas, extended a long arm, and hauled him up. The wind buffeted Tomas as he stood and watched Eduard sobbing in his father's arms, nearly inconsolable.

"He should have come home," Eduard gasped. "He should!"

"Aye, son, I know. We loved him dearly, and your grief is shared by all of us. We cannot argue God's will, and we cannot bring Maddox back by attacking one who I suspect was very dear to him. The best you can do is go on and step up into the place that was meant to be his. Do you understand, lad?"

Eduard nodded his head. Lady Joan picked her way forward and mopped his cheeks as she might those of a small child. "Son, do come inside. We are all of us overwrought."

The servants filed away, following Lady Joan and her maid, who looked stricken. Lady Joan had her arm around Eduard.

The driver took charge of Algernon. Tomas and Lord Hugh were left facing one another.

"My lord," Tomas began. "About Mistress Genevieve—I did not intend... I would never take what belongs to Maddox."

Lord Hugh sighed. "What did once belong to him. She is his betrothed no more. I love the girl like a daughter. How can I do aught but wish her happiness? If that happiness lies with you—"

Tomas bowed his head, struggling with his emotions. "It does not, my lord. It cannot be. She blames herself for sending Maddox on that quest, even as I do blame myself for what happened to him. Had I fought better that day, he would not have been captured. Had he not been captured, he might never have taken the fever that stole him from you. It is as Eduard says—my fault."

"And he may have taken the fever while at the Church of the Holy Sepulcher, speaking prayers for Genevieve's father. We cannot say. You must forgive Eduard. He is, as was said, overwrought. Come inside and get warm after that terrible journey. You are still welcome to lodge with us a while."

"Lord Hugh, your kindness proves how Maddox came by the generous spirit that was so much a part of him. I do not think I can."

"You can scarcely travel back to Clarendon tonight." Lord Hugh quirked an eyebrow. "Will you return to Clarendon?"

"I had not planned to do so, my lord."

"Well, that is something which can be decided another day. Come inside now, and be our guest."

It seemed the height of discourtesy to argue it further, and Tomas did not wish to keep Lord Hugh standing longer in the wet and cold. Following him inside, however, was the last thing he wanted to do.

He dragged his heavy boots a bit and glanced back at Algernon. The driver tipped his cap. "Not to worry, sir, I'll take fine care o' him."

"I will send a crew of men back to bring the wagon and oxen," Lord Hugh said as they passed into a large entryway, one far grander than that at Clarendon. Tomas caught no sight of Lady Joan and Eduard. A serving girl busily mopped up the melted snow they had left behind, and a man, most likely Lord Hugh's seneschal, hurried forward to greet them. "My lord."

"Master Timothy. Sir Tomas, come." Lord Hugh led the way into a comfortable side chamber where a fire was already being laid.

The seneschal said, "Lord Hugh, we did not know when you would return, so this chamber is not yet warmed."

"It soon will be. Pray, bring us something hot to drink and sort some clothing for Sir Tomas."

"Sir," the seneschal looked questioning.

Lord Hugh cleared his throat. "Some of Master Maddox's things will no doubt do."

"But, no." Tomas turned to Lord Hugh in distress. It was too much. "His things? I could not. I am sure I have some extra clothing in my pack."

"The things in your pack will be soaked clear through. My son would not mind. Allow us to do this as I believe Maddox would wish."

Again Tomas could do nothing but bow his head.

"And, Master Timothy," Lord Hugh went on, "sort out a bedchamber for Sir Tomas, where he may wash and refresh himself."

"My lord."

Things had got away from Tomas. He had no choice at all.

****

The mulled wine tasted like heaven, going down.

Tomas, who remained soaking wet, stood in front of the fire to imbibe, and the seneschal soon returned to lead him off to his chamber. He left Lord Hugh staring, brooding, into the fire.

The seneschal led the way up a wide flight of stairs to a landing where the walls were painted in patterns of flowers and stars. They paced a hallway that overlooked the entry below to a door at the far end.

"Master Maddox's room, sir. You will be most comfortable here."

Before Tomas could balk, the man led him in.

"I will send the lass up to lay a fire. Master Maddox's things are here." He went to a clothes press. "I am sure, as Sir Hugh says, he will not mind, and the room is going spare till he returns."

Tomas gazed at the man in surprise. Had he not been a member of those servants outside, and if so had he not heard or understood Eduard's accusations? If not, how could he know that Maddox had perished in the Holy Land?

"I regret to tell you, Master Timothy, Master Maddox will not be returning home. I brought word that he perished in the Holy Land."

The man paled and wobbled so severely Tomas feared he might fall. "Nay! Were you—were you with him there, Sir Tomas? In the Holy Land?"

"I was."

"Oh, woe! This is a loss, a terrible loss. All of us were most fond of the young master."

Tomas bowed in acknowledgement of the man's grief. "Understandably."

"By heaven, this will—well, it will devastate the master and mistress."

"*Oui*." And their surviving son.

"Please, use whatever you need from the room. If there is anything more I can procure for you—"

"I have all I need."

The words were a lie. Even as the man hurried out, Tomas, standing there chilled to the bone in his muddied boots, knew of one thing—one person—he needed most terribly and could never see again.

Because whatever Maddox's father said, Genevieve still belonged to the man who commanded the loyalty of every heart in this house.

****

Always before, prayer had brought Genevieve a measure of peace. Even when Father had been so ill, when she could feel him slipping from her relentlessly, a visit to the chapel had restored a measure of comfort. It felt like placing at least a half measure of her troubles in someone else's hands.

Now, though, she stared blankly at the rose window above the chancel, kneeling until her knees ached. No words, no prayers came. The terrible desperation did not ease.

How had it all come to this? Bad enough losing Father with his cheerful nature and steady wisdom. Worse seeing how it had affected everyone else, especially Mother. But she'd had to pull herself together then, to keep the household organized and running smoothly.

She'd expected Maddox to return. On some level, she'd accepted they would eventually marry. He—and his family—would take some of the burden from her.

She had done all she could for her father. In his death there had been great sadness but no guilt.

In the loss of Maddox lay both. And so much despair in her present situation, her heart struggled to beat.

She blinked at the rose window and tears trickled down her cheeks. She did not know what to do for young Ralph and his sister, how to save them. What if the sickness spread? What if they lost still more members of their household?

They lived close here at Clarendon and knew one another so well. What were they but family?

"What should I do?" she asked the silent, freezing air of the chapel. But no answer came. She struggled to her feet, moving like an old woman.

Should she try to send for the physician? But, even now, snow once more fell outside. A cruel winter and a bitter one this proved to be.

Should she let the fever run its course?

One thing she absolutely knew she could not do, and that was think of herself. Her wishes—her desires—did not matter now, if they ever had.

And that meant she could not let her thoughts stray to the tall young man with the head of black curls and the fervent gaze. She could not ponder how it made her feel when he looked at her with those dark, earnest eyes. How, even from the first moment when he'd knelt at her feet to present the mistletoe heart, he seemed to have touched her very soul.

Above all else, she could not allow herself to relive the kiss, the single kiss they had shared. The warmth of it. The thrill. The sense of belonging that had blossomed inside her.

She had a duty to perform—moreover now, with Father gone. And she had penance to pay for betraying Maddox's love.

Chapter Twenty-Four

Tomas would have liked to avoid wearing Maddox's clothing, likewise using his wash basin and his comb. But Lord Hugh was right. All his own things were wet, the damp having soaked clear through the pack in which he carried them.

He had to believe what Lord Hugh and the seneschal said. Maddox would not mind what he borrowed. Had they not shared every gulp of water and scrap of food that had come to their cell? The water had been especially prized. What was a shirt or coat by comparison?

The most fair-minded of men, Maddox would have denied him nothing.

Except, perhaps, the beautiful woman of whom his heart sang.

Maddox had never left off speaking of her, praising her. How sweet her spirit. How kindly her smile. The beauty of her eyes and the ease he felt always in her company.

All true. Hearing all that, and listening with sympathy—for he had never been in love—Tomas himself had more than half fallen in love with her before he met her.

Maddox had cared for his Genevieve so deeply, so truly, and done all he could to make her happy.

Tomas remembered a moment near the end, when

Maddox had been lying on his heap of straw, burning with fever, and had asked, "What could I do but answer the request of her heart and come upon this journey? If I could complete the pilgrimage and save her father's life for her—how could I ever refuse?" His fingers had clutched at Tomas's. "But I have failed. I failed her."

"You have not failed her, my friend. You are here, at great cost and sacrifice."

"What if her father does not survive because of me?"

If there were any mercy at all, Maddox would never know that Lord William had perished near the same time he had.

And now Tomas stood here in Maddox's home. In his place. In his clothing. How was he to live up to that?

The young girl came to light the fire in the bedchamber, her eyes red with weeping. When Tomas made his way downstairs from Maddox's chamber, he found that each person he encountered looked the same. They had shared the news, then, and their reactions showed just how beloved Maddox had been. Indeed, it honored the generous man all the more.

Tomas found Lord Hugh in the hall, which proved a larger but less comfortable chamber than the one at Clarendon. Here a fire blazed and a meal had already been laid out.

Tomas went at once to Lord Hugh and said, "I hope you will forgive the slip of my tongue that shared the news of Maddox's fate with your seneschal. I could not allow him to keep hoping for his young master's return."

Lord Hugh gave a pained smile. "Indeed, you have done me a good turn. I did not know how I would share the dire news with them. Sit, sit. My wife has taken to her bed and will not be down."

"And Eduard?" Tomas asked with caution.

Lord Hugh's expression turned grim. "Ah, Eduard. I will tell you frankly, Sir Tomas, young Eduard always envied his elder brother a bit. Maddox was set to inherit the estate, and life came so easily for him. He was bright, well-spoken, and loved by everyone he met. The golden child, if you will." He sighed. "Eduard has always been more difficult, more prone to turning sullen, and resistant to correction. And now, the one he resented—and whom I am certain he loved most dearly—is gone."

"Clearing the way for him to inherit the estate," said Tomas, beginning to see. Would he feel that way if something happened to his elder brother? If he in turn became something more than an afterthought to his father? It seemed all three of them—he, Eduard, and Genevieve—experienced a measure of guilt.

"Aye," Lord Hugh said softly. "I think he is merely placing his own feelings upon you, Sir Tomas. He does not blame you for Maddox's death, not truly. None of us does."

Tears came to Tomas's eyes. He bowed his head. "You are too kind. Too forgiving."

Lord Hugh hesitated. "My wife—she has taken all this very hard indeed. And she is a mite upset over what Eduard related to us about yourself and Mistress Genevieve." He shot Tomas a close look. "Genevieve occupied Maddox's heart for so long, from the time he was a young boy. He never had any doubt that she should be his bride. It is a difficult thing for my wife to accept, that Genevieve might look favorably upon another."

"My lord, I want you to know I will not be returning to Clarendon again and will not see Mistress Genevieve anymore."

"Are you certain of that?"

"*Oui*, so you might share that with your lady wife, and give her comfort."

"Ah." Lord Hugh seemed to ponder it. He poured two goblets of wine, and handed one to Tomas before lifting his eyes to Tomas's face. "I feel that would be a terrible pity, and a shame."

"Eh?" Astonishment washed over Tomas, so strong it stole any further words.

Lord Hugh's mouth creased in what might be a sad smile. "Mistress Genevieve is a fine young woman, one whom I love already like a daughter. Should she grieve and suffer lifelong because Maddox did not make it back from the Holy Land?"

"I think, my lord," Tomas had to clear his throat, "I think she believes she deserves little because she sent him there."

Lord Hugh's gaze did not waver from Tomas's when he said, "I believe she deserves exactly what Maddox would want her to have. And that is happiness. Can you provide her that happiness, Sir Tomas?"

"My lord, I do not know."

"It is something, perhaps, for you to discover. Now come, drink your wine. The night is bitter cold, and we all have a measure of that cold, or so I believe, lodged within. But we are safe and warm here tonight. We should be grateful."

Tomas was. Ah, *oui*, he was.

They sat by the fire and dined together, while Lord Hugh asked Tomas questions about himself. "Tell me more of the young man who proved such a good friend to my son. You say you are from France."

"From Brittany, my lord."

Tomas spoke to distract Lord Hugh, and out of gratitude for his kindness. He spoke of the estate near the coast and of his father's fierce nature. "He is a knight to his very bones, and demanded his sons follow after him. It was either that or the church for me. While I am devout, I could not see that life, or retiring from life, as it were." He'd always wanted a family of his own, a wife of whom he might grow fond and a crop of children with whom he would never be harsh. For whom he would not set bars impossibly high to leap.

"When I heard that the three kings—our own King Philip, your good King Richard, and Frederick of Germany—had determined to join together and reclaim the Holy Land for Christians, I decided to join. I thought that might at last please my father."

"And did it?" Lord Hugh asked sympathetically.

"Yes, it seemed to, very much. He arranged for me to join the company of his friend, Sir Herbert DeFougeres, and even as you did for Maddox, sent several members of the household guard with me." Tomas faltered. "Those guardsmen all lie dead now."

"What is he like, this Herbert DeFougeres?"

Tomas smiled. "I like him very much, and respect him even more. He is a fierce warrior for *le croix*, but he also has a heart." Sir Herbert had been able to see why Tomas needed to withdraw from his company and follow a higher duty to England, one owed to a dead man.

"What did he do to free you from your captivity?"

"Everything he could. He did manage to free me in the end, through negotiation. I refused to leave without Maddox. But it was too late for him."

Lord Hugh reached out and clasped Tomas's hand. "I will be forever grateful you did not allow my son to languish and die in chains."

"Sir Herbert and all the company were most grieved we could not save Maddox. Even in the short time they knew him, well—" Tomas struggled for words. "There was a sweetness in him, was there not?"

"That is the truth. Tomas, you are welcome to stay here for as long as you wish. Your horse is safe and cared for in my stables, and I am cheered by your company. You must stay at least until the weather clears. After that, you have a long journey ahead of you." Again Lord Hugh's gaze met Tomas's. "If indeed you intend to return home."

"So I do."

"What do you think your father will say when you arrive home?"

A good question. Tomas's father might greet him with rage over his abandonment of his place with Sir Herbert. Or with disgust. Tomas did not know which would be worse.

"I cannot say, Lord Hugh, except that I fear I will prove a disappointment to him."

Lord Hugh examined Tomas with a kindly eye. "One thing I have learned—a man should cherish his son while he may."

"I do not expect to be cherished, *non*."

"You are welcome to stay here—for good, if you will."

"*Merci*." Tomas stared at him, astonished. "It is kind in you. But I do not think that would be a good plan, with Eduard needing to find his feet."

"Perhaps not. But give yourself time to ponder the matter. As I say, the roads may keep you here yet a while." Lord Hugh hesitated. "Or, I suppose you could always return and rejoin this Sir Herbert's company."

"It is without doubt what my father would expect." Tomas thought of the arduous journey back to the Holy Land, the burning sun and tortuous conditions.

He thought of Genevieve DeClare.

"I must consider on it," he agreed, "and discover just where my duty lies."

Chapter Twenty-Five

When morning came, Genevieve rose with a feeling of dread. It had snowed again yesterday afternoon and evening, coating the stable yard she must cross in order to treat Ralph and his sister, Elspet.

She could only hope Lord Hugh, Lady Joan, and Eduard had reached home safely and were in their manor house before the icy precipitation had resumed on the roads.

She hoped Tomas, having seen them home, would return. Return to her.

But why would he, over such treacherous roads? Besides, had he not told her he intended to move on? To return home to his duties in Brittany?

She could not expect to see him again.

The children were no better this morning. Genevieve struggled to convince herself they were no worse. But the breath rasped in young Ralph's lungs, and the rash had crept like a flush up little Elspet's cheeks.

Their mother had clearly not slept. She bathed their faces with cool water as Genevieve had instructed and stark fear lay in her eyes.

"Mistress, am I going to lose them?"

"Only God can say, Rachel." Again, Genevieve wished she could call for a physician. She cared nothing for the expense, but last night's weather had served to worsen rather than improve the roads.

When she went back inside, she found the household in disorder. Mother stood in the hall, wringing her hands. Gilliane had refused to leave her chamber. Agnes and her family had come down to table as had Uncle Gervase. But there was no breakfast.

Gervase intercepted Genevieve when she entered the hall. His pale gray eyes engaged hers gently.

"The cook's son has taken ill."

"No." All the breath went from Genevieve in a rush. "Not the same illness?"

"I fear so. I have not seen the child, but I have spoken with your cook. She is frantic."

Genevieve's mind spun. "They play together all the time, Benedict and Ralph."

"Aye."

"I must go and see the boy."

Uncle Gervase laid a hand on her arm. "My dear, your mother and I think you should not."

"But there is no one else. With the roads as they are—"

"Let his mother tend him. If, indeed, some dire sickness has been brought within these walls—"

She stared at him. "You suppose that Sir Tomas brought it."

He shrugged. "He came directly from the Holy Land where all manner of sickness abides. Moreover, he came from the side of Maddox, who harbored just such a fever. Who can say if he carried it hence?"

"But Uncle, Sir Tomas was not ill."

"He was not, when he left here. Who can say what has befallen him since?"

Cold terror gripped Genevieve by the throat. By the heart. She could not lose him, this man who had come so unexpectedly into her life. She could not.

"My dear..." Uncle Gervase's gaze softened to one of kindness. "I know what you are, with your soft heart. And I know you mean well, wishing to care for those of this household. But I beg you to be cautious. I do not think your poor mother could withstand losing you so soon after your father's passing, and after losing young Maddox, of whom she was so fond."

Genevieve nodded. "Aye."

But what was she to do? Allow the children to languish? To die? Who was she, that her life must be considered above theirs? Were they not all as good as family?

She did not want to distress Mother, no. Yet Tomas, without fear, had not hesitated to hold Maddox while he died.

Could she do any less?

A dilemma, for certain.

Agnes came and put an arm around her and led her to the table. "Your dear mother has gone to the kitchens and will ask Cook's helpers to prepare us something. Come and sit down."

"I am sure I can eat nothing."

"You must try."

Lord Roger, young Justin, and Emmaline already sat at the board, looking unaccustomedly subdued. A stab of alarm passed through Genevieve's heart.

Like Cook's son, Justine and Emmaline had played with Ralph in the snow.

She clutched Agnes's hand. "Are your children quite well?"

"They say so."

Genevieve glanced down the table. "And no one else

feels ill?"

Roger shook his head. Master Dennis, who sat by the fire, said nothing.

Genevieve tried to reassure herself. Master Dennis had not been in the stable yard. And he appeared well.

After the kitchen maids had brought pottage and bread, Genevieve lost all control of her concern. "I must go and see Benny."

"Allow me." Uncle Gervase arose with a sigh of capitulation. "I will go up with you."

The upper reaches of the house seemed uncannily quiet. Genevieve remained in the corridor outside the servant's room where Cook hovered over her son's cot, whispering prayers, while Uncle Gervase went in.

The prayers, as so often, did little good. Uncle Gervase soon returned, his face pale.

"Uncle?"

"He is quite ill with fever." Gervase's gaze encountered hers. "I fear we must somehow send for a physician."

There was sickness in the house, a most unwelcome guest.

****

Genevieve and her mother together spoke to both footmen. The journey to Scarborough, the nearest market town that would harbor a physician, was a perilous one. Despite the distance, the best method of travel would be on foot.

Both young men stood before them, strong and tall.

"I would send you both," Mother told them, "for safety's sake. But I cannot spare the two of you. Wilfred?" She eyed the more strapping of the two.

His companion, John, spoke up. "My lady, I will

go." He flicked a look at his fellow. "Wilfred likely will not tell you, but he says he has a sore throat."

Genevieve stared in horror. *No!* Ah, and what had been visited upon their household? Was it a punishment for the thoughts she'd harbored? An answer for her guilt?

Mother spoke softly. "Then by all means, Wilfred, you must stay here. John, if you would be so good as to undertake the journey—"

"Aye, my lady."

"Dress warm. Are your boots sound? Genevieve, where are your father's good boots? We will lend them to the lad."

"My lady!"

"The way is so far, John, and the roads will be filled with snow. Genevieve, where is your father's heavy cloak? We will give him that also, and I will fetch a measure of coin, John, for you to show the physician."

Mother hurried off. Genevieve stood gazing at the two earnest young men who, as she knew, were close in age and mightily fond of one another.

As fond, perhaps, as Maddox and Tomas had become.

"John, I wish you did not have to travel alone. But needs must."

"Aye, mistress."

"Wait here while I fetch my father's cloak and boots. Wilfred, you are for your bed."

"But mistress!" He waved his hands in distress. "I am needed at my post."

"Aye, so you are, which is why we want you to recover as quickly as ever you can."

"There will be no one to look after ye, mistress."

"Then we shall have to look after ourselves for a

short while." Kindly, she told him, "Be sensible, now."

"Aye, mistress." But he certainly did not look happy about it, and he eyed his companion with regret.

"You take care out there, John, mind."

"You know me. Too smart to fall in a puddle and drown."

Chapter Twenty-Six

John had not yet left when Lord Roger came to Mother with Agnes at his side, his usually lively expression turned grim.

"My lady, I hear you are sending one of the footmen for the physician."

"Aye, Lord Roger."

"To Scarborough? If so," he added with regret, "we would like to take the opportunity to accompany him. 'Twould be a help to him, to travel in company, and an advantage to us also, to have a strong young man on hand should we bog down."

"You wish to leave, you mean? So soon?" Genevieve, who stood by, exchanged a look of distress with Mother. "But it is not yet Three Kings Day."

"And the roads are very bad," Mother pointed out. "Surely 'twould be better to wait for them to clear."

Roger and Agnes exchanged a look. "We intended to," Sir Roger said. "But with the children at hand—best perhaps to risk the roads rather than having them fall ill."

Her Christmas celebration was falling to pieces, Genevieve thought. Why had she even made such an ill-fated attempt?

Roger urged, "If you allow your footman to travel with us, I will direct him to our own physician, who has long attended my family."

Mother glanced again at Genevieve. "That would

indeed be an advantage."

"It would," Genevieve could only agree.

Mother asked Roger, "How soon can you be ready to travel?"

"An hour."

"I will inform John." Mother hurried off, and with a nod, Roger went to attend to his preparations.

Agnes turned to Genevieve. "Oh, Cousin, I am sorry. We had meant to stay, certainly. But I can only agree with Roger that a house that harbors sickness is no place for the children."

"To be sure." And how would Genevieve feel if either Emmaline or Justin fell ill? Still, her heart lay heavy in her breast.

Seeing her expression, Agnes stepped up and embraced her. "Take heart, Genevieve. Things are not so dire as you fear."

"Why do you say so? Our Christmas celebration is in tatters. Those for whom I care are ill. And—"

"Perhaps he will return," Agnes whispered in her ear. Her blue eyes looked kind. "If the feelings between you are genuine and strong—"

"I do not believe Sir Tomas will return. And if he did, what should I do with the guilt?"

"My dear." Agnes brushed Genevieve's cheek with gentle fingers. "I did not know Maddox as well as you did. I did meet him over the years, however. He did not strike me as the sort of young man who would wish for you to punish yourself for something that was not your fault."

"But it *was* my fault." Genevieve's gaze clung to her cousin's. "I sent him."

"And did you put him in that horrible prison? Did

you give him the fever that stole his life?"

"No." But she might as well have done.

"Do not despair," Agnes urged. "In this life, many things can happen. Bad can follow good, surely, but good can also come out of bad."

"Aye."

"I am sorry to be leaving you in your time of uncertainty."

Was there any uncertainty in it? Genevieve was very certain she should not love Sir Tomas, even if her heart refused to listen. And certain he would not return to Clarendon, no matter how she might wish him to.

"Go safely." She embraced Agnes in turn. "And keep well. Look after John for us."

Agnes laughed. "I am hoping we will look after each other. He can lodge with us when we arrive home. Roger will notify the physician."

"That is a blessing."

"Blessings are many, and here is another for you." Agnes kissed Genevieve on the forehead. "Now I had better join Roger before he begins to fret."

The house grew emptier and emptier, Genevieve thought sometime later as she stood watching Agnes and her family depart. First Father had disappeared from it. Then she had learned Maddox would never visit here again. Tomas's departure with the DeVilles had struck deep. And now her cousin's family with John, a member of their own.

It hurt her heart.

"Uncle..." She turned to Gervase after they'd watched his daughter's wagon rumble and splash away down the drive. "Tell me you do not plan to leave us."

"That I do not. These old bones are much too achy

and fragile to brave the roads in their current condition. I will stay for as long as you need me."

Genevieve brightened. "Do you mean that? I think it would gladden Mother ever so much."

"I do not doubt that both you and your mother would benefit from a steadying hand, since your father's death. Not that you, my dear, have not managed very well. You have. But until you marry—"

Genevieve's face went tight. "I do not know that I ever will, Uncle."

He strove to sound jovial. "Of course you will. You are young yet. And linked to a grand estate. If you like, I will help your mother to make the arrangements."

Noting her expression, he held up a hand. "Not yet. To be sure, you need time to grieve the loss of dear Maddox."

"There has been so much grief."

"And not enough joy." Uncle Gervase turned to the harper who had just come into the chamber with Rex at his heels. "Master Dennis, do you care to play at Alquerque? You may keep me company with endless games of it. Two old men together, eh?"

"Certainly, Lord Gervase."

"It is well. Please excuse me, both of you. I wish to check on Wilfred and the children."

"My dear, I ask you again to keep a careful distance."

She would if she could. But she was needed here, and no mistake. The prospect of marrying, however— marrying a stranger—caused her to go breathless.

She could not. She simply could not. Not while remaining in love with Tomas Monmercy.

And did she truly love him? Were the emotions she

felt toward him real, and not just the product of how handsome he was, how valiant and kind? Of the gallant way he'd thrown himself at her feet?

Would she still love him if she never saw him again?

Aye, so she would, with a helpless, heedless longing that would follow her to the grave. That did not make what she felt for Tomas right. But it did make it all too genuine.

Chapter Twenty-Seven

Contrary to Tomas's expectations, Lady Joan smiled when she saw him in her son's clothing, a watery smile to be sure, but sincere. "It is good to see Maddox's things getting good use. I am glad, Sir Tomas, that you may benefit from them."

He bowed. "My lady." He could say no more. Her generosity of spirit made sense, when he thought about it. Maddox had possessed the same. There had not been a selfish bone in his body.

However, when the household servants restored his own clothing, he was quick to don it. He folded Maddox's things away reverently in the press from whence they'd come. That did not change the fact that he found himself sleeping in Maddox's bed, on the very pillow where he had laid his head. Or that, at table, he sat in what he suspected had been Maddox's place.

The entire circumstance was indeed monstrously awkward, and though he did not encounter Eduard at any of the meals, that young man failing to make an appearance, he lived in dread of doing so. He felt restless, and eager to leave. But where to go?

The roads remained difficult. The prospect of traveling all the way to the port at Sutton and thence to Brittany did not appeal. Even less did he welcome the prospect of returning to the East and rejoining Sir Herbert's company. That would be his father's choice for him, without doubt. Tomas could only imagine his *pere*'s expression of disgust if he arrived home ahead of Herbert's company.

The truth was, he did not want to go home. Oh, he loved the land itself and appreciated the beauty of the nearby sea. He cherished memories of the days when he had run free there with his sisters and brother, and played at being knights. But things had changed. There was no more play. His brother, Philippe, was heir to the place Tomas loved.

Worse, it seemed Philippe had taken on his father's opinions of him. By the time Tomas left home, there were no more smiles, there was little shared laughter. Philippe would soon wed and produce heirs of his own, who would oust Tomas still further.

No, he did not want to go home. He wanted to return to Clarendon.

Impossible. But he could not stay here either, no matter how kind his hosts.

The restlessness drove him out to the stables to visit the amiable Algernon. Lord Hugh's men had managed to drag in the wagon and team marooned the previous day, but if anything, the roads looked to be in even worse condition.

He could travel by stages, if he wished. South. Brittany lay south. So, much nearer, did the DeClare estate.

He warred with himself over it. 'Twould be better— easier perhaps—never to see Genevieve DeClare again. To never catch the sweep of black lashes over pale gray eyes. The coming and going of emotions on her face, like flickers of light. The hover of a smile upon sweet pink lips.

Oh, those lips that he had kissed. Better, *oui*, to cut the cord of longing that connected him to her, quick and clean.

He had accomplished his duty to Maddox. Time to take up his former duty and return to the Holy Land.

Maybe he would lose himself there, perish in the heat, the dust, and the blood of battle. If a man had no future, his worries must end.

****

How long before the physician might arrive? Genevieve pondered it a score of times. As she strove to spoon broth into children who were burning up before her very eyes. As she listened to poor Wilfred rave from his narrow bed. She even prayed over it in the chapel, when she could steal the time.

Not soon enough, she concluded. The journey to Scarborough for John and her cousin's family would be slow and perilous. Then there was the equally perilous journey back to Clarendon. She did not know if her charges could hang on that long.

At least no one else had fallen ill. She watched the household closely, these individuals whom she loved. Mother concerned her the most. But even though she appeared so frail, there remained an iron core within her, and she did not waver. Moreover, Cook did not fall ill even though she'd been living with and tending her son.

Genevieve did think Master Dennis appeared a bit unwell, as if he'd begun to unravel at the seams. Perhaps he but felt weary following his long stay. He but rarely played upon his harp, though he did provide Uncle Gervase with an opponent at Alquerque, as promised.

When Genevieve inquired after him, he replied only that he fared well enough.

Gilliane presented a far different problem. She had taken to her bedchamber and steadfastly refused to come down, even for meals. Out of concern for her health as well as her emotional state, Genevieve eventually presented herself there.

An unwelcome guest, as it proved. Gilliane opened the door of her chamber but reluctantly, and when she saw who waited there, her expression shut down tight.

"Let me in, Sister," Genevieve requested.

"I do not want to talk to you. I do not want to look at you," Gilliane answered waspishly.

Ignoring that, Genevieve brushed past her. "Are you feeling well?"

Gilliane glared at her. "Well? How could I feel well? I am angry, and upset, and feeling the grief for Maddox that—that you plainly do not."

"How can you say that?" Genevieve turned to face her sister. "You know not what lies in my heart."

Gilliane's chin tipped up. "I know you did not love him."

Tears flooded Genevieve's eyes. "I did, most dearly."

"I do not believe you. Had you loved him, you would never have exchanged a kiss with Sir Tomas. I saw you! You quite likely thought yourselves lost in the shadows of the entry, but I saw."

"I will not deny I have feelings for Sir Tomas. Strong feelings. I loved Maddox most sincerely and deeply, Gilliane, but perhaps not the same way he loved me. I was not in love with him. But my grief is real and heartfelt."

"Are you in love with Sir Tomas?"

Tears filled Genevieve's eyes. She turned away. "It

does not matter. I will never see him again."

Gilliane said nothing.

"You will think it a fitting punishment, no doubt. What I deserve for sending Maddox on the pilgrimage that ended his life."

"You never should have sent him."

"You are right. I should not. It was selfish of me and not what he deserved." Genevieve repeated it softly. "Not what he deserved."

"It is not fair. That he should have loved you so, when I—" Gilliane stopped speaking abruptly. All at once she started to cry. After a moment's hesitation, Genevieve took her sister into her arms.

"It is not fair." She could but agree. "None of it. Please believe I never wished him harm. And even if you find a way to forgive me, I will never forgive myself."

Gilliane nodded.

"Now pray, Sister, come downstairs. Mother needs your company. My time is taken with nursing those members of the household who remain unwell."

Gilliane raised brown eyes awash with tears. "What if you fall ill?"

"Perhaps that, too, would be my fitting punishment."

"Nay!" Gilliane's arms came out and clutched at Genevieve. "I do not want anything to happen to you. Anyway—" She choked on her tears. "Eduard will take care of it."

"Take care of it? Whatever do you mean?"

"He told me he meant to answer Sir Tomas as he deserved—perhaps even on the road to the DeVilles' estate."

Genevieve stared at her sister, aghast. "But Sir

Tomas has done no wrong!"

"Eduard believes he should have fought harder and saved Maddox from his fate. 'Tis why the knights are in the Holy Land, is it not?"

"Treachery? Do you say he intends treachery?"

"Well, aye, so I do believe."

Genevieve flew down the stairs. She found her uncle in the hall, and poured out the accounting to him. "We must do something, Uncle! You must go after them. Give warning—"

"Genevieve." Uncle Gervase got to his feet. "My dear, it will be too late. They will have reached the DeVille estate yestere'en at the very latest. Sir Tomas will either have warded off any attack Eduard intended, or be—"

"Do not say it. Do not say it!" Genevieve begged.

Her uncle looked at her kindly. "He means a very great deal to you, this young man."

Genevieve did not answer. She did not need to.

"Oh, my dear, take heart. Sir Tomas is a hardened knight. A stripling lad, even one in training, is no match for him."

"A knife in the back requires little skill. If Sir Tomas is not expecting an attack—"

Uncle Gervase did not speak.

"I will never know," Genevieve lamented, in a hush. "Since I will never see him anymore, I will never know if he is dead or alive."

"You will. Surely Lord Hugh will convey to us any news, once the weather permits."

Uncle Gervase did not understand. Each moment of parting from Tomas was an agony. Days of not knowing what had befallen him would be an ordeal surpassing what she could endure. But endure it she must.

****

Somehow, Genevieve made her way through the rest of that day, caring for her patients and ignoring her own pain. When her throat began to ache, she strove to ignore that also. She had no other symptoms besides feeling tired, and she had a right to that, as she'd been doing much to spare others, particularly Mother, from tending the sick.

When a headache joined the raw soreness in her throat, she told herself she often took headache from the wind. When, while undressing herself that night, her maid being otherwise occupied, she saw the rash beginning on her chest, she lost all her breath on a gasp of despair.

No. She could not fall ill. She simply could not. She had too much to do. She had a household to hold together.

She sank down on the stool in front of her dressing table and wrapped both arms around herself. Perhaps a strong will could fight off the illness. Perhaps by doing so, by carrying on, she could atone for the mistakes she had made.

She unwrapped her arms and reached for the carved box on the dressing table. Inside lay not only the mistletoe heart she had fashioned for Maddox—the one that had traveled all the way to the Holy Land and back again—but the sprig she'd taken down after Tomas kissed her.

Magical, that kiss had been. She lifted the sprig from the box and pressed it to her lips.

Protect me, please. And oh, Tomas, return to me. I need you more than I can say.

She tucked the tiny treasure safe away beneath the fold of silk that enwrapped the mistletoe heart. She must hope her maid did not see the blush of red that crept up her chest. She must keep this secret close to her, and carry on.

Chapter Twenty-Eight

A thrush sang deafeningly from the eave outside Tomas's window and wakened him. The first light of morning had just broken, and the bird greeted it with a full heart.

In defiance of the weather.

Tomas lay in the comfort of Maddox's bed, his eyes wide open, and wondered when he'd last heard birdsong. All manner of birds had abounded at home, flickering through the fruit trees, soaring out to sea. But they seemed to have been lacking in the Holy Land, and he held his breath while he listened to this one tumbling out clear, liquid notes.

He had been dreaming. Dreaming he'd been back in the barren cell with Maddox.

That young man had drawn from the pouch where he kept it, close against his chest, the mistletoe heart. His blue eyes clear and earnest in his overly thin face, he held it out.

You must go to her. Genevieve's happiness is more important to me than anything else. It is my most fervent aim and dearest wish.

But Maddox had never said that, in life. He'd spoken endlessly of his Genevieve, true, enough to make Tomas long to meet her. But not until after they'd been freed and he lay dying of the fever had he urged Tomas to return the heart to his love.

"Tell her I tried. I tried, but I failed. I am sorry." That, he had said.

"You did not fail, my friend. And if she knows your heart, she knows the courage that lies there."

Go to her.

Those words from the dream echoed in Tomas's mind. *You must go to her.*

Even though Tomas lay warm in the bed, a chill chased its way up his spine. Had that been a message sent via a dream? What did Maddox know that Tomas did not?

He had intended never to return to Clarendon. The break had been made, and that was the hardest part. Or so he'd thought. It appeared living without Genevieve, or living with her in his heart while he could not be with her, was harder still.

What if she needed him?

Go to her, Maddox seemed to whisper, *as I cannot.*

Mon dieu, I am losing my mind. And no surprise, if true. The ordeal in Saladin's prison had taken much from him. He had refused to think then of himself and had focused on Maddox. But the confinement, the deprivation, and the frequent beatings had cost him dearly. They'd both been walking skeletons when Sir Herbert got them free.

He'd been proud then that he had not broken, in his mind or his courage. Neither of them had. But he could admit now that Maddox's subsequent death had broken something in him.

He'd focused on completing Maddox's journey for him and bringing Genevieve the mistletoe heart. He hadn't intended to fall in love with her.

Perhaps—perhaps only now did he unravel. It must

be so, if he saw Maddox in his dreams and heard his voice in his head.

Go to her.

So he had. He had covered uncountable miles to reach the young woman with the sweet smile. He had surely fulfilled that duty.

Then what was he doing here in Maddox's bed, in Maddox's place? If, as the bird argued, he might travel again, he needed to leave and take up his own life.

He was not Maddox or indeed a substitute for him. He did not love Genevieve with Maddox's heart but with his own. He needed to take up his life.

He arose, dressed, and went out to visit Algernon in the stables. The great war horse greeted him with a nose over the half door of his box.

"We have been cooped up long enough, eh?" Tomas asked the horse. "What do you wish to do?"

He imagined Algernon wanted to get out of the stable and down the road. He did not suppose his mount pondered the difference between sailing home to Brittany and returning to the Holy Land.

"This very day," he promised the horse, "we will go."

Lord Hugh protested when Tomas announced his decision. "But young man, I and my lady wife hoped you might stay."

"It is kind in you, especially given the circumstances. I regret I cannot stay. Things are awkward with young Master Eduard, and—"

"He is sorry, to his heart, for what he has done."

"I do not doubt it." Tomas had to struggle for words when he went on. "My presence here can only serve to provoke ill memories for all of you."

"That is not so. And I hope you will return some day to see us. You will forever be welcome."

Tomas bowed his head. "Please bid Lady Joan farewell for me. And Master Eduard also."

"I will. And Sir Tomas, may God go with you."

****

The roads had firmed up from what they'd been when Tomas and the DeVilles journeyed from Clarendon. Algernon picked his way between the ruts and the high places, in good spirits. The morning proved clear, and from the height where the DeVilles' manor house stood, Tomas could see for miles southward.

The world, after all, was a beautiful place, even here in England. The land stretched away before Tomas in undulating waves, a patchwork leading to the far distance. He must journey even as did the three kings whose day approached so swiftly. He needed to think of the future and not his own heart.

Go to her, Maddox whispered in his ear.

Non.

All at once the beautiful morning disappeared from before Tomas's eyes. He was once again back in the cell, and it was night, the only light they had that which bled down the corridor from far beyond. Just the two of them. Alone. Feeling forsaken.

Tomas sprawled on his back, his one longing that for a draught of water. Cool, clean water—not the scant measure of thick, swampy stuff they were provided, far too seldom, to share.

Weak and beaten, he wanted to give up. To close his eyes. To stop wanting.

Maddox clasped his hand.

"You must be strong. We will get out of here.

Somehow."

"We will not."

"Come, Tomas. You are the one who has kept me believing."

"I want water. *Mon Dieu*—"

"You want to live. One of us must."

That had never happened. Maddox had never said that to him.

"Listen to me, Tomas. She needs you. She needs you now."

The vision cleared from before Tomas's eyes. He found himself once more surrounded by the bright morning.

Algernon had come to a halt. Rather, Tomas must have drawn him up unintentionally.

Or perhaps very intentionally.

A track, a turning, lay to his left. In worse condition even than the road, it lay adrift with the remnants of the last snow, and so rutted a man could disappear up to his knees.

The path to Clarendon.

Tomas's heart began to pound, and his hand tightened on the reins. Algernon's head came up obediently.

Tomas glanced away south. Home lay there. Duty.

Go to her.

With a sound in his throat that might be a sob, Tomas directed Algernon down the path toward the castle.

Chapter Twenty-Nine

Hold on, Gennie. He is coming. He is on his way.

That could not possibly be Maddox's voice Genevieve heard in her ear. But it must be. No one else ever called her Gennie, not even her parents.

Only her dearest friend.

But oh, she was afire and burning up. Her very world felt aflame. A raw ache held her throat fast in its grip, and she felt too weak to rise.

When had she taken to her bed? She'd been so determined not to let on she felt ill. Not to any of her charges, or their parents. Not to Mother, most assuredly, or to her uncle, who began to look at her with concern.

Instead she'd kept right on administering draughts, bathing her patients' heads, even while her own ached so she could not bear the pain.

When—? Ah, she remembered now. She'd collapsed into her bed after looking after everyone else, and when the gray light of morning crept past the mullions she'd lacked the strength to rise. She dimly remembered her maid coming, peering at her, and exclaiming in dismay. Hurrying away to fetch—

Mother? Had Mother come?

She hoped not. She needed to tell them all to stay away, only she felt certain that, with her throat hurting this way, she could not speak.

But aye, she dimly remembered Mother being here

in the chamber, looking shaken. And Uncle Gervase. Certainly not Maddox. He could not in truth have spoken any words in her ear.

She let her eyes stray around the chamber, making sure she was for the moment alone. It looked the same as always. The outside walls hung with tapestries to fight the draft. The single window. The chest over against the opposite wall, the clothes press.

Nobody, nobody there beyond the bed hangings.

The chamber blurred before her eyes, and she shut them in self-defense.

And heard Maddox's voice again.

Gennie, you must be strong. Be stubborn as you have always been. Even now, he rides to you.

"Who? The physician?"

But she knew. Of whom would Maddox speak, if not the man who had suffered and bled along with him?

He who had brought her the mistletoe heart.

Somehow, she opened her eyes again. She saw no one.

"Maddox?" she whispered, but it was barely a word, coming through her enflamed throat.

Her door creaked open and Mother rushed in, followed by Uncle Gervase. Her uncle drew up a stool. Mother sat beside the bed and took Genevieve's hand. Genevieve could see she'd been crying.

"Oh, my dear, my dear girl! Gervase, how long before John returns with the physician?"

"It cannot be soon enough, Maude."

"I cannot lose her, Gervase. I will not."

"Then hold her fast, and pray."

It seemed Genevieve could hear the prayers. Fervent and devout, they spiraled up and filled the air of the chamber. Did they go any farther? Did they reach God's ears? Or Maddox's?

Her maid, Maureen, came in with a basin and began bathing Genevieve's head the way she'd been doing for others these many days.

Genevieve lay feeling helpless and thinking about the fact that nothing had gone the way she'd hoped during this holy season. She'd wanted to gladden Mother's heart and lift her from her grief. She'd longed to recreate the season Father had loved so well. Now she lay here while Mother wept.

Do not despair, Gennie.

I have lost Christmas, she thought at her best friend.

You have not. There is still time.

She struggled to add up the days in her mind. Christmas Eve, when Tomas had arrived.

Tomas.

The wild longing in her heart overwhelmed her, and her own tears came. She could not number the days. She had lost too many in comings and goings, in tending the sick.

She remembered the kiss. The pure, strong sweetness of it. The feeling of being in Tomas's arms. The pounding of his heart beneath her fingers. One kiss to carry her through a season. Through a life.

I am sorry, Maddox. I am sorry it is not your kiss I treasure. I am sorry, so sorry for everything. Can you forgive me?

He did not answer, and for an instant she thought he had abandoned her. She could still hear Mother praying, and Maureen's soft breaths when she leaned close with her cloth to bathe Genevieve's head.

Then, softly, his voice rustled in her ear. *There is no*

need for forgiveness between us, Gennie. Not ever.

But I sent you away. I did not love you as I should.

You loved me as you could.

And do yet! And will forever. Stay with me.

I will.

If I need to make the walk into paradise, walk with me.

I will.

Is that why you are here?

A clatter sounded from below. Mother abandoned her prayers to look at Gervase. "Is that the physician? Pray go and see."

He went out. It could not possibly be the physician. It was far too soon.

Maddox whispered to her, *He is come.*

****

One of the serving girls opened the door to Tomas and stood shivering in the cold. Overhead, clouds raced before a wind sharp as a knife.

Where was the stout footman?

"Sir Tomas?" the girl looked astonished to see him.

She made no move to let him in, which he found passing strange.

From behind her came hurrying footsteps. Lord Gervase appeared.

"Young man?" He appeared as astonished as the servant. "We did not expect to see you again so soon."

"My lord, I did not expect to be here." *My heart has brought me.* But he could not say that. "I—I wished to say another farewell before I continue my journey south."

Gervase took the serving girl's place at the door. His dignified face wore lines of distress. "There is sickness in the house. You had better not come in."

"Sickness?" Genevieve?

"Aye. We have sent for the physician. He cannot arrive soon enough."

"And the ladies here?"

"Lady Maude and Mistress Gilliane are well. Mistress Genevieve lies gravely ill."

Tomas's world rocked around him. He swore he felt the stones upon which he stood tilt beneath his feet.

"Lord Gervase, I would still beg admittance."

"Aye, lad—I understand. You will have to care for your own mount. Several of the servants, including young Ralph, are down."

Not Ralph. Not Genevieve!

"I can surely care for my own mount."

"Then go stable him and come in by the kitchen."

"I will."

Gervase shut the door. Tomas led Algernon away through the bailey and into the stable yard, which lay strangely bare of all but snow. With each step, his heart hurt more dreadfully within him.

He led Algernon to his old stall in the stable. No sooner had he settled the great horse than the ostler, Roderick, came hurrying in, hair wild and lacking his coat.

"Sir Tomas. My lord, things here are dire, indeed."

"I have heard." Tomas searched the man's stricken countenance. "Ralph?"

"And our wee Elspet also. My lady Genevieve was tending them ever so kindly. But now she has fallen ill herself."

"What sort of sickness is it?"

"Fever and an ache of the throat, Sir Tomas."

Cold struck Tomas from his heart downward. The same as had stricken Maddox. The very sickness that had taken his life.

Chapter Thirty

Roderick continued speaking as Tomas finished settling Algernon and gathering his gear.

"My Lord Gervase's daughter and her family have left, gone home, and neither of her young ones ill even though they did play with my Ralph. You are Ralph's hero, you are, Sir Tomas." Tears filled Roderick's eyes. "Having been all the way to the Holy Land and back again, and fighting for Jerusalem the way you did. It would do him that much good to see ye, but I'll not ask ye up." He jerked his head at the quarters above the stable.

"Roderick, how ill is he?"

The tears spilled over. "Hard to say, Sir Tomas. I always thought he'd take my place here after me—"

"So he will yet, Roderick. Take heart. He is a fine ostler already, at his tender age."

"Cook's lad is ill also. And Wilfred—"

An unfortunate situation, indeed. At the very least, Tomas thought as he crossed the yard on his own and let himself in through the doorway to the kitchen, he might help out with some of the tasks that must be going undone with so many down sick.

He passed the yawning doorway of the kitchen where only a few maids worked, and continued to the hall, where he found Master Dennis, the harper. The man sat alone at the table, nursing a mug of ale, but perked up when he saw Tomas.

"Sir Tomas." He got to his feet. "I thought 'twas yourself I heard at the door. Then again, I might have been mistaken. The house is all in an uproar."

"So I have heard." Tomas deposited his bag and weapons near the wall and joined the harper, whom he eyed closely. "Pray, tell me all."

"Sit and have some ale. Since there is no one else available, I will play host. The ostler's children fell ill first, then the cook's boy. The footman. And then Mistress Genevieve."

"How bad is it?"

"Bad enough, by all accounts."

Even though he'd already heard it from Gervase, Tomas asked again, "Can you tell me the nature of the illness?"

"I can, aye, only too well. Weakness. A burning in the throat. Fever. A rash."

Tomas breathed again. "A rash? What sort of rash?"

"I can show you." Dennis folded back the sleeve of his shirt and showed the inside of his forearm, where a series of red prick marks populated the skin.

Tomas stared. "You? You have contracted this illness?"

"Aye. Do not get too close. It is much better than it was. The pain in my throat is nearly gone—doused it with ale, I have—and the rash is receding."

"But why do you sit here, *monsieur*?"

"I did not tell anyone I'd fallen ill, and I beg you will not either. These good people who did offer me a roof this holy season have enough to worry them with their own. Who am I but a wandering minstrel?"

"You should be in your bed."

"I have suffered worse ills upon the road. I tell you, it is retreating from me."

Tomas put his head in his hands. "I feared when I heard there was illness here that I had somehow brought it. From the Holy Land." From Maddox.

Dennis eyed him from across the table. "A long way to carry sickness and not contract it yourself."

"*Oui*, but—Maddox. He had such fever. And the pain in the throat. No rash."

"Aye, well from what I have heard, all our present sufferers from the oldest to the youngest do have the rash. So I expect that exonerates ye, eh?"

"Exonerates?"

"Clears ye from any blame. 'Tis but an illness such as springs up in the winter."

Tomas looked at him again. "And, *monsieur*, you have done nothing to fight it? Merely sat here?"

"Sat here, aye. Tended the fire since there was no one else. Drank ale."

"How much ale, *monsieur*?"

"My good young sir, I hate to tell you."

****

Lady Maude came down from her post in Genevieve's room sometime later, accompanied by Lord Gervase, and wept to see Tomas. Pale of cheek and with shadows beneath her eyes, she had clearly been keeping a vigil.

Tomas went to one knee before her. "My lady, I have heard of the sickness in your house. Only tell me what I may do to help."

"Dear boy. We are beset, and no mistake. I am so very glad to see you. Come, sit with me."

Tomas arose but asked, "Mistress Genevieve—how

fares she?"

"Caught fast in the fever, Sir Tomas." Lady Maude dabbed at her eyes. "She speaks to those I cannot see. To Maddox."

Tomas spoke to Maddox also, upon occasion, but did not say so.

"Her skin, it burns beneath my fingers. I do wish the physician would arrive, but I do not suppose, given the state of the roads, we can expect him so soon."

Gervase led Lady Maude to the table and Tomas followed, resuming his former seat. He shot Dennis a look before he said, "I have seen such fevers."

Lady Maude looked stricken. "In the Holy Land?" Tomas thought he saw the reflection of Maddox in her eyes.

"And elsewhere, m'lady. It is well to provide the sufferers much to drink." Something he had not been able to do for Maddox.

"We have offered her wine. She can swallow little and will take even less broth."

"And young Ralph, and his sister? Your footman?"

"The same."

Tomas exchanged another look with Dennis. "You must try offering them ale. As much as they will hold."

She stared, as did Gervase. "And this will make a cure?"

"It will not hurt. Do you have sufficient ale in the house?"

"We had just finished brewing for the holy season. Genevieve—Genevieve wanted there to be plenty for her guests." Two tears ran down her cheeks.

"That is well."

Dennis lifted his tankard from the table to his lips.

"I would listen to him, my lady. All the ale they can hold."

Now Maude and Gervase exchanged a look. Gervase said, "'Tis most certainly worth a try."

"Lady Maude, may I see Genevieve?" Tomas asked.

"I am not sure that is proper."

"My lady, I care little what is proper. I have come back because—" He had no words to finish the thought.

Lady Maude blew out a breath. "Aye, lad. We have lost enough already, all of us, have we not? You have arrived on the twelfth day of Christmas, just like the three kings. Our blessed mother did not deny them a chance to visit our Lord. How can I deny you?"

Gervase reached across the table and patted Tomas's hand. "Let us try your cure first, eh? We will begin with young Ralph. I will myself take a flagon out to the stables." Kindly, he added, "Will you come with me?"

"*Oui*, my lord."

Better that, by far, than to sit and wait.

Chapter Thirty-One

Young Ralph and his little sister, Elspet, lay in their parents' bed, tucked up so tight only their heads could be seen. Tomas felt overly large and clumsy, clomping in on his boots. Elspet slept fitfully, as he saw when he approached the bed. But Ralph peeled open his eyes to look at Tomas.

"Sir Tomas." It came out as no more than a croak. "Algernon?"

"Safe in the stable downstairs." Tomas smiled at the boy, even though dread gripped him. This looked bad. The last time he had seen someone so ill…

But no, he would not let himself think of that.

Like Mistress Maude, Roderick's wife did not appear to have slept. Her hands trembled when she gestured to her children.

"We have done all we can, Lord Gervase. Bathed them. Warmed them. Doused them with every cure available to us."

"My good woman, I have one more cure for you to try." Gervase hefted the flagon of ale.

"Ale?" Roderick faltered.

"But they cannot swallow," his wife protested.

Tomas told her, "I beg you only to try."

Roderick and his wife exchanged glances. She nodded brokenly.

"Ralph first," Gervase instructed. "Roderick, will

you lift him up?"

Tomas whispered a prayer as Roderick gently propped the boy up on his arm. A measure was poured into a cup. Ralph gulped it down greedily. Gervase poured more.

"There now," Roderick said when both children had been dosed, Elspet taking her portion without truly awakening. "At least he may sleep for a time."

Ralph's eyes were still open. He gave Tomas a smile before he closed them peacefully.

"Let us move on to dose Wilfred in his chamber," Gervase suggested.

They found Wilfred in the small chamber he shared with John, tended by one of the kitchen maids.

"How fares he?" Gervase asked her.

"His fever still burns high. The rash may be receding from his chest, so. See?"

She turned back the blankets and then the collar of Wilfred's night shirt. Small dots of red covered his chest.

"Those were all the way up his neck."

"Has he taken anything to drink?"

"Precious little, my lord Gervase. He tells us his throat hurts too much."

"Let us get a measure of ale into him."

This time, Tomas held the patient, Wilfred being a big man, while Gervase administered the doses. As Ralph had, Wilfred drank eagerly and soon after fell asleep.

"It may well ease his pain," Gervase said to Tomas, "and thus let him find rest."

"Who would think," asked the maid, "the cure would be such a pleasing one?"

****

Tomas was not permitted to see Genevieve quite yet. Like the other patients, she was dosed, and her mother stayed by her side thereafter.

Left alone with Dennis the harper, Tomas asked him, "You are feeling better, are you, Master Harper?" The sparkle had returned to the man's eyes.

"Very much so. And grateful to have a warm fire beside which to spend this season. And…" He smiled. "Plenty of ale."

"You are certain all you did to cure yourself was drink the ale?"

"Aye. You do realize, Sir Tomas, you will get the credit for this cure if it does its work."

Tomas shook his head. "I am more than happy to lay credit where due, at your feet."

"Nay, I bid you accept it. What better," Dennis wondered, "to win the heart of a beautiful young lady than to let her believe you have saved her life?" He smiled. "I suspect you have already won her heart, though."

"You speak of Mistress Genevieve?"

"She is beautiful, is she not?"

"I have no reason to believe she regards me with other than ordinary kindness." Except for that kiss. There had been that kiss—

"Ah, well, Sir Tomas, you did not see her after you had left. The sadness in her eyes, the droop to her shoulders."

Tomas smiled reluctantly. "You are a poet, I think."

"It is indeed part of my profession. But in this, I am most sincere."

"Master Dennis, I am sure you have heard the story. She was betrothed to another, who loved her right well, as well as any man could love a woman."

Dennis's gaze turned serious. "Master Maddox. I have heard, aye. And 'tis a tragedy such as those of which we troubadours sing. He did love her well. Have you asked yourself if she loved him also?"

Tomas lifted his hands in a gesture of helplessness. "How could she fail to so love him? A fine man, earnest and sincere. As fine as any I have ever met."

"Ah, and being so, what would he want for her now? To grieve endlessly? Or to find her happiness?"

Tomas had no question, in his heart. "Still," he whispered, half to himself, "I may have brought the illness that threatens her and all those here."

"As might I. As might Lord Gervase himself or those who traveled from Scarborough."

True enough.

A silence fell, during which Tomas listened to the fire crackling in the great hearth. Dennis took another drink of ale before he spoke again.

"My lord, allow me to tell you something. I have lived longer than you—by God, I dare say twice as long—and have seen many things. Learned a good bit also, on the road. One thing I have learned is that there is no use in us flagellating ourselves over things we cannot help or change. And certainly no good in punishing ourselves for those things. Happiness is fragile. As fragile as—as that heart you brought Mistress Genevieve from the Holy Land. It must be cherished, when found."

"You are a wise man, Master Harper." Tomas gave him a burning look. "And I think I am very glad we met here by chance."

"My good young sir, I do not believe in chance. Do

you truly think we came here so? It is something else I have learned. We are directed whence we are meant to be. Especially," he tapped his ear, "if we follow our inner music. Speaking of which..." He arose, just a bit unsteadily, and reached for his harp, which stood against the wall. "I think I feel recovered enough to make a song. One for Mistress Genevieve."

He began to weave a delicate tune while Tomas sat and listened. The enchanting music arose like the sparks from the fire, each note a separate thing of beauty.

Could Tomas argue with anything the harper said? He could not explain why he and Maddox had been in the same place at the same time, in Jerusalem. Why they had been taken prisoner together. Held in the same cell. Formed a friendship made from equal parts sharing and need. One that might have spanned years instead of days.

He had half lost his heart to Genevieve before ever he saw her. And when he did see her—

Were such things indeed meant? He could not deny Maddox had directed him down the snow-clogged lane back to Clarendon.

Maddox, of the generous heart.

Suddenly Tomas wanted to weep as he had not since a young child. Such pain lay in it and, just like one of the harper's tunes, such beauty.

Was beauty enough? As he sat there nursing his mug of ale, Tomas wondered. Not the beauty of form or face, for although Genevieve certainly possessed both, he found they meant little more to him than the softness of a summer's day. But the beauty of spirit Maddox had brought right into their grim cell when he spoke of her.

And the radiance of Maddox's own spirit.

My friend, I would not take what you loved, no

matter how generously you have led me back to her.

No answer came, only the exquisite notes trembling upon the air.

Chapter Thirty-Two

They played together in the orchard once again, Genevieve a lass of no more than nine or so and Maddox not much older. The summer had passed, and autumn turned the sky a deeper blue. The apples had nearly all been harvested. Only the windfalls remained and, heated by the afternoon sun, gave off a heady fragrance like wine.

When the two friends came here, and they did so often, Maddox always searched out a couple of windfalls that were mostly unblemished and not yet plundered by wasps. One was for Genevieve to eat and one for himself. If he found but one, they shared it bite for bite.

Genevieve was not supposed to be here, running wild with her dearest friend, the neighbors' lad. Mother said she was too old for it now and should be at her lessons, or working at her needlework like her older sister, Anora. She would no doubt get in trouble when she reached home later.

It was worth it.

She eyed the young lad who swung his agile body around the limb beside her, his hair the color of ripe hay swinging over his forehead each time he spun. Would Maddox get in trouble too? He'd already ruined his jacket, and dried leaves clung to his hose.

His parents adored him, and though they might have a few words for him later, Genevieve did not imagine the scolding would be severe. Nor would her own.

They were blessed.

Sitting there on the branch of the apple tree with her feet dangling a number of yards off the ground, she knew they were blessed.

Their parents loved them. Everyone loved Maddox. She did, herself.

He righted his body and sat on the branch beside her before giving her a grin. Wide and sunny, it reflected the quiet joy in his blue eyes. She just had to smile back at him.

"Let us stay here forever," she said impulsively. "Let us never go home."

"I would like that, Gennie, above all things. But I cannot remain for long. I am dead."

Dead? She stiffened on the branch and her nails dug into the bark. "That is not funny, Maddox."

"I am not trying to be funny. It is so."

"How can you be dead? You are right here beside me."

His gaze turned serious. "I will always be with you, Gennie. Because I love you. Here."

He dug into his pocket where she saw a bulge the size of an apple. He had found another for them to share for, to be sure, her friend—her very best friend—was not dead. She could see him. Smell the sunshine on his skin. Mark the dirt under his fingernails.

He hauled his hand from his pocket and extended the object he held to her. It was not an apple.

It was the mistletoe heart.

She gazed from it, frayed and tattered on his palm, to his face. He no longer looked like a young boy. He'd become a man, but not the man she'd sent away from her, the man she'd sent to Jerusalem.

His face had gone thin and gaunt, as worn as the object on his palm. His clothing too showed signs of hardship, and bruises marked his skin. But a steady, true light shone in his blue eyes.

"Here, Gennie. Take it. It's yours."

She stared, unable to move.

"I was unable to bring it back to you as I wished. So I sent it with another. He is a good man. Only I know how good. I would have liked to know him longer as a friend. But I gift him to you. Here. Take it."

Blindly, for tears filled her eyes, Genevieve held out her hand. She felt the skin of Maddox's palm brush hers as he dropped the trinket into it.

"I would have liked to marry you myself. 'Twas all I ever wanted. But I do believe another is destined for you. I thought at first, there in the Holy Land, I had failed you."

"No, Maddox. No. 'Twas I who failed you."

"Gennie, listen. I learned some things, there in that cell, about love and sacrifice. I learned that, even more than I wished to marry you, I wanted you to be happy. He can make you so."

Genevieve could barely see him at all now, for the tears. "Forgive me, Maddox. Forgive me. I never should have sent you away." She bowed her head, swamped by guilt and remorse.

And felt his fingers brush her cheek. "Aye, you should. How else might I have found him for you? He has a good heart, Gennie. Just as you deserve."

"Forgive me. For—"

"Gennie, look at me."

Stricken, she raised her eyes. "You must lay this

malaise aside. Arise and go to him. Give him that."

"Nay, Maddox. This heart is yours. This, I will treasure forever."

He smiled. "Go, Gennie, and live your life. Be joyful in it. I will see you anon."

I love you. She did not speak the words aloud. There was no need. He had gone, and she found herself no longer in the sunny autumn afternoon. It was winter, and she stood there in the snow, alone.

Without him, the dearest friend of her heart. But had he truly gone?

No.

The fragile, woven heart still lay in her hand. With tender care, she closed her fingers around it and turned back toward the castle, and home.

Had she the courage to do what Maddox asked? Pick up the pieces of her life? Go to Tomas with an open heart? Forgive herself?

Because now she saw the truth. Maddox had forgiven her. On some level, she'd always known he would.

Much, much harder was forgiving herself.

Tomas deserved better than this chill that had taken up residence in her heart. And perhaps, just perhaps, Maddox deserved a better return on his sacrifice.

She stiffened and shivered when someone spoke her name. A cup was tipped against her lips. The snow-strewn orchard dissolved around her, broke up into pieces. She lay in her own bed.

"Drink," Mother said again.

"What is it?"

"Ale. Oh, my darling girl, our Wilfred has returned to us. And all three children have slept long and deeply, and awakened on the mend. You must drink."

Genevieve's throat opened. She drank. "What day is it?"

"Three Kings Day. And Sir Tomas has returned. A blessing."

She was blessed.

Genevieve sought her mother's eyes. "He is here?"

"He is."

Genevieve opened her clenched fingers on the coverlet. She did not hold, there, the mistletoe heart. Of course not, for it rested in the small box where she'd stowed it. That one would forever belong to Maddox.

Yet she did have a life to live. And a love to bestow.

"I want to see Sir Tomas."

"Sleep first, daughter, and then you will."

Chapter Thirty-Three

The morning after Three Kings Day dawned bright and beautiful, without a hint of snow. Tomas, who went out early to care for Algernon, stood for several moments observing the rose-gold light that came streaming over the hills to the east and warmed the stones of the castle walls.

Inside the stable he met Roderick, who greeted him with a wide smile.

"Sir Tomas, 'tis a joy to see ye on this fine morning."

"And you, Roderick. How are the children?"

"Mending well, sir." Roderick's smile grew wider. "They've had their skins full of ale, and no mistake. Ralph's woken up hungry and his sister not far behind him. Her rash has fair faded away."

Tomas blew out a relieved breath. "I am very glad to hear it."

"Cook says her boy's doing well, and I hear tell Wilfred's back on his feet." Roderick's gaze grew serious. "And 'tis all down to you, sir."

"Not so. 'Twas Master Dennis the harper who gave me the idea."

"Still and all, sir, we are that glad to see you returned. And you may be sure your big war horse will get the very best of treatment at our hands."

"All the horses here get the best of treatment."

"I am back at my duties, and Ralph soon will be. You may go in, sir, and enjoy your breakfast."

"Thank you, I will."

Tomas met Lord Gervase in the hall. The strain of the days just passed showed in wear on that man's dignified face, but he too broke into a wide smile upon sighting Tomas.

"My good sir, we are that pleased to have you returned. Come in to breakfast. You must be hungry."

Tomas was not eager to break his fast or to spend time speaking with Gervase and the harper, no matter how well he liked them. He most certainly did not wish to encounter Gilliane. His one thought centered upon seeing Genevieve. But he sat down with Dennis and Lord Gervase, the only ones present, and made a good show of it.

When they had nearly finished, Lady Maude came hurrying in, her face alight.

Tomas got to his feet. "My lady. How is Mistress Genevieve?"

Lady Maude's eyes shone. "Awake, and better. I believe she would like to see you." Tomas abandoned his breakfast without a backward look. He did not notice as Lord Gervase and the harper exchanged smiles.

"Come, and I will take you to her."

****

On the stairs outside the solar, they encountered Mistress Gilliane, making her way down. The young lady looked far different from the defiant and angry girl Tomas had first met. Now she came with eyes red from weeping, her hands clasped before her, but with a measure of relief dawning in her face.

To Tomas's utter surprise, she reached out to him,

one of her hands closing on the sleeve of his doublet.

"She is better, better this morning. I sat beside her bed all night, Sir Tomas, and I prayed. Oh, how I prayed! I blamed her because, well—" Her brown eyes met Tomas's, "—because Maddox favored her, instead of me. And because she sent him away. But I see now that we all do and say, sometimes, what we should not."

"So we do, mistress."

"Genevieve did not intend to send Maddox away to die. Indeed, 'twas a perilous journey, but others have made it. You have, yourself. She would never have sent him if she thought he would not return."

"Gilliane—" Lady Maude began.

"Nay, Mother, I must say this. It was unfair, Sir Tomas, for me to blame you, any more than her, and not right for me to encourage Eduard DeVille to attack you." Her gaze searched his. "He did not succeed in his plans, on the way to the DeVille estate?"

Lady Maude gasped.

"He did not," Tomas assured the girl. "And we have made our peace."

"I am glad. That is all I prayed for last night, a chance to make my peace with Genevieve. Go to her. Go to her now. She deserves her happiness."

He nodded, and Gilliane hurried past him down the stairs.

Lady Maude looked at Tomas in turn. "What did happen on the way to the DeVilles' estate?"

"My lady, it does not matter now."

She nodded, and led him to a door that stood open, with morning light spilling out through the aperture. She gave him a tremulous smile and ushered him in.

The room looked a comfortable one. A dressing

table and bench stood to the left near the single window, a clothes press to the right. Straight ahead was the high bed with the draperies all drawn back.

Genevieve lay in the bed. She rested against an embroidered pillow with the coverlet up to her chin and her hands free upon it. And oh, by the blessed virgin—

She wore a cap, but beneath it her hair flowed loose, a curtain of black silk. Maddox had spoken of her hair— how it flared out when she'd climbed one of the trees in the orchard as a child, or chased after him. Tomas had, of course, never before seen it, as a proper lady kept her hair covered in company.

He'd never seen it, *non*, but he had pictured it in his mind.

He went to the side of the bed, feeling overly large in this feminine place, and went down on one knee beside it, just as he had the first time he saw her, in the great hall.

His heart already lay at her feet. Could he do otherwise?

"My lady." He bowed his head. He needed her to know he came to her humbly, without expectation.

She touched his hair. Her fingers slipped through the curls that tumbled over his brow, and she urged, "Sir Tomas, look at me. Please."

He raised his head and lost himself in her eyes. Pale gray between fringes of black lashes, they glowed like the morning. And what he saw there—

For him? Could that be for him?

"My lady, how are you?"

"I have been ill, and I have to admit I feel passing strange. I do not know how much ale my good mother tipped down my throat." The expression in her eyes changed. "I slept, Sir Tomas. I dreamed."

"Sleep may provide a cure for many things."

"So it seems. I am glad, very glad you have returned."

"I am glad to be here, more than I can say. If I brought this illness that has beset you, from my travels, or from the Holy Land—"

"You have brought me many things. Not that."

Reaching across the coverlet, she twined her fingers with his. Tomas glanced at the door to see how her mother might react to this, and saw that Lady Maude had gone, leaving them alone.

He clutched Genevieve's fingers tight. "Mistress Genevieve, when first I came to Clarendon, it was at the urging of duty. I brought you Maddox's heart then, all the way from the Holy Land. He was the best man I ever knew, and possessed the truest spirit."

Tears flooded her eyes. "He was the best man I ever knew also. I suspect—I suspect he still is my best friend. Is it possible that, across all those miles, he sent you to me?"

"He wanted only, ever, for you to be happy." Tomas raised her fingers to his lips.

"And," she whispered, "will you agree to stay here at Clarendon, and make me so?"

Tomas struggled for words against the emotions that filled him. Ardent devotion. A lifetime's worth of love.

"Genevieve, I once brought you Maddox's heart. Now please let me offer you mine."

"Aye." She smiled tremulously into his eyes. "Oh, aye. But we will have to wait until spring for the wedding."

"As you wish. But why?"

"Our wedding must be held in the orchard, amid the new blooms."

"*Mon Dieu.*" A wedding held outdoors? An unusual prospect, as unusual as this woman and her family, who had opened their doors to accept him as a second son. Not on the basis of his rank or nationality, but on the value of who he was inside.

"But why?" he asked again.

"Because I want Maddox to be there. What better witness might we have than the one who brought us together?"

She was clearly still a bit confused, his dear one. Tomas pressed her fingers to his heart. "I will strive always to live up to his faith in me. And yours."

"I believe you," Genevieve said softly. "And as you and I know, my dear one, 'tis all about the believing."

A word about the author...

Multi-award-winning author Laura Strickland delights in time traveling to the past and searching out settings for her books, be they Historical Romance, Steampunk, or something in between. Her first Scottish Historical hero, *Devil Black*, battled his way onto the publishing scene in 2013, and the author never looked back.

Nor has she tapped the limits of her imagination. Venturing beyond Historical and Contemporary Romance, she created a new world with her ground-breaking Buffalo Steampunk Adventure series set in her native city in Western New York.

Married and the parent of one grown daughter, Laura has also been privileged to mother a number of very special rescue dogs, and is intensely interested in animal welfare.

Her love of dogs and her lifelong interest in Celtic history, magic, and music are all reflected in her writing. Laura's mantra is Lore, Legend, Love, and she wouldn't have it any other way.

Thank you for purchasing
this publication of The Wild Rose Press, Inc.

For questions or more information
contact us at
info@thewildrosepress.com.

The Wild Rose Press, Inc.